Anna Wilson has two black cats called Ink and Jet. She was always a Cat-Type Person until she got her gorgeous black Labrador, Kenna. Now she is a Cat-AND-Dog-Type Person, and she keeps chickens and a tortoise too. She has just about enough space in her house for her husband and two children as well. They all live together in Bradford on Avon in Wiltshire. Anna has written many young-fiction titles for Macmillan Children's Books and plans to write many, many more!

Books by Anna Wilson

The Great Kitten Cake Off
I'm a Chicken, Get Me Out of Here!
Monkey Business
Monkey Madness: The Only Way Is Africa!

The Pooch Parlour series
The Poodle Problem
The Dotty Dalmatian
The Smug Pug

The Top of the Pups series
The Puppy Plan
Pup Idol
Puppy Power
Puppy Party

Kitten Kaboodle
Kitten Smitten
Kitten Cupid

And for older readers
Summer's Shadow

www.annawilson.co.uk

TOP
of the
PUPS

Pup idol

Anna Wilson

Illustrated by Moira Munro

MACMILLAN CHILDREN'S BOOKS

First published 2008 by Macmillan Children's Books

This edition published 2015 by Macmillan Children's Books
an imprint of Pan Macmillan
a division of Macmillan Publishers Limited
20 New Wharf Road, London N1 9RR
Associated companies throughout the world
www.panmacmillan.com

ISBN 978-1-4472-7982-2

1 3 5 7 9 8 6 4 2

A CIP catalogue record for this book is available from
the British Library.

Typeset by Nigel Hazle
Printed and bound by CPI Group (UK) Ltd, Croydon CR0 4YY

For Kenna —
the One and Only Pup Idol

Contents

1
How to Tackle Behavioural Issues

I hope everyone out there will know by now about how I, Summer Holly Love, finally persuaded my mum to let me have a wonderful puppy all of my own called Honey.

That's me!

And how my annoying and embarrassing older sister, April, tried to steal her so that she could get a date with the vet Nick Harris – and, most importantly, how my best friend,

Molly Cook, and I (oh, and Mum in the end, I suppose) came up with a Masterly Plan to get April her date and get Honey returned one hundred and ten per cent to ME, her Rightful Owner.

If the Reading Public do not yet know all this, there is no excuse: it's all there in *Puppy Love*, the fascinating and frankly terrifically gripping account about how I came to be a very responsible and loving dog owner . . .

. . . of a very cute pooch.

Anyway, things have Moved On since those early days of dog-ownership. For a start, April and Nick are Going Out, which apparently means they Stay In and watch telly – and

KISS. URGH! This means that the sitting room is almost always Out Of Bounds, so I am finding that I spend more time out in the garden or the park with Honey.

And then there's the fact that my puppy Honey is actually *not* so much of a teensy-weensy puppy any more when you look at her. She is still a very cuddly and cute thing, of course, and she is not fully as big as an adult dog, but she *is* growing and growing by the day. I sometimes think that if I had the time to sit and watch her every second of every minute (and I really wish I could do this, but Real Life keeps getting in the way), she would actually grow before my very own eyes! Just like one of those little foam bath toys you can get that positively explode growth-wise the minute you drop them in the water.

At any rate, I have been taking pictures of her once a week ever since we got her,

3

and when I had a look through them on the slideshow thingy on the computer, it was *exactly* like a cartoon ANIMATION of a dog getting huger and bigger at a very high speed. So that's how I know how much she is growing.

Now, I don't know whether this is connected to her getting bigger, or whether it is just her own cheeky personality TRAIT, but I have noticed that as well as growing in a Physical way, her naughty habits have been getting rather larger too.

Hey!

But of course she is still adorable. And anyone with ears as soft and velvety as Honey can get away with most things in life. (If they are a puppy, that is. A person with soft and velvety ears would just be gross.)

In fact, Honey is so adorable and has

become such an important Part of My Life that
she recently came very close to knocking Molly
Cook off the top spot of best-friendship. It was
a terrible and difficult time, which involved
lots of cross words (as in 'being angry', not
a puzzle in the newspaper — although those
are so difficult that they sometimes make me
have a terrible time too). In fact, at one point
I thought I would never have any friends ever
again . . .

All of this started
with Honey becoming
a bit of a handful
and developing A
Mind Of Her Own.
She seemed to have
become totally
deaf when I called
out any of the
commands I had taught

her when she was small (not that she was *that* brilliant at listening then, but at least she tried) and instead would go off and Do Her Own Thing.

I'm one crazy kid!

For a start, she would leap and jump about all over the place and not come when I called her. It was most distressing and was beginning to make me feel quite sad, as I realized that I was losing the Special Bond that I had had with Honey when she was a tiny little cuddly puppy that I could just pick up and hold in my arms.

Well, I certainly could not do that any

more. Apart from growing, Honey had become really quite strong. Sometimes when we were out for a walk she would forget she was on the lead

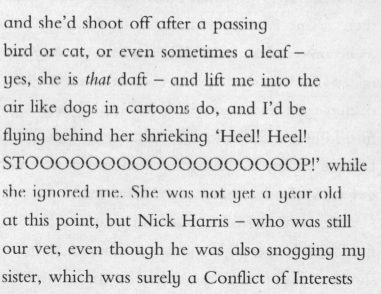

and she'd shoot off after a passing
bird or cat, or even sometimes a leaf –
yes, she is *that* daft – and lift me into the
air like dogs in cartoons do, and I'd be
flying behind her shrieking 'Heel! Heel!
STOOOOOOOOOOOOOOOOOOOOP!' while
she ignored me. She was not yet a year old
at this point, but Nick Harris – who was still
our vet, even though he was also snogging my
sister, which was surely a Conflict of Interests

Under the Trades Descriptions Act – said that she would carry on growing until she was a year and a half old.

'Holy Shmoly!' said Molly, which is one of the things she says if she is shocked or surprised. 'If she carries on growing at the same rate, she'll weigh, oh, at least fifty kilos by the time she's one!'

Molly normally knows every fact there is to know about everything, but I have to say that there is one Area of Life in which I happen to be more of an EXPERT, and that is dog-related facts. Anyone with even a small amount of dog-type knowledge will tell you that fifty kilos is a ridiculous weight for a female Labrador. But I didn't think I should point this out to Molly in case she got offended.

Anyway, however much Honey would finally end up weighing, it was obvious that she was going to keep getting bigger, so unless

How to Tackle Behavioural Issues

I learned to train her better I was DESTINED to be a Laughing Stock among dog owners – and probably anyone else who saw me walking her in the park as well. I could see it now: me being pulled off my feet by Honey; us bumping into Honey's mum, Meatball, and her stinky owner, Frank Gritter; and *him* guffawing in an uproarious manner and bellowing, '*She's walking in the air!*' in an out-of-tune RENDITION of that famous *Snowman* song. It was not an image that bore too much thinking over.

On top of all this, Honey had developed some pretty weird and horrid habits around the house. First of all, she had taken it into her

 head to eat shoes. REAL SHOES. She had decided that she liked nothing more than a tasty bit of slipper or trainer for a snack. That particular habit really got out of hand when Honey ate one of April's best flip-flops.

Yum and Yummier!

'I can't stand that mutt!' April screamed, when she discovered Honey with the remains of a gold flip-flop strap hanging out of her mouth. Poor Honey did not know what she had done wrong.

Was she saving it as a snack for later?

'I've told you all about Honey's shoe FETISH,' I explained calmly to April. 'If she gets hold of a shoe, it's *your* fault, April. You should not leave them lying around.'

For some reason Mum nearly choked on her cereal when I said this.

I felt like also telling April that it was not Pleasant to say 'mutt' (which is an ugly word), especially because if it hadn't been for Honey, April would never have got together with her Beloved Nick. But I thought that might be pushing things a bit.

Instead I said, 'Honey's just becoming an Awkward Adolescent. You know – a teenager. She's going through a Bit of a Phase, that's all.'

Mum really did choke then, and had to run to the bathroom. On the way she squeaked something about April having been an Awkward Adolescent herself in her Dim and Distant Past.

★

11

There were other, more terrible incidents that
Mum in particular didn't find at all amusing,
like the time that Honey jumped up and pulled
the Sunday roast down off the kitchen table
when Mum had gone to the door to let in
some guests.

And the time when she chewed April's new
mobile phone.

And the time she ate the birthday cake that
Mum had just made for April.

12

And the totally weird time that she pulled all the dishcloths out of the sink and shredded them around the kitchen.

Dishcloths are a rare delicacy, in my humble opinion.

So all of this made me think that I probably needed to find out more about training Honey so that could I find a way to tackle what Molly had started to call Honey's Behavioural Issues and get back to having a Special Bond with my dog.

I decided I should talk to Mum about this, as I thought, being a grown-up and everything, she might have some useful advice on the matter. So on the way home from school one night, I practised in my head how I might start this conversation. (I do this a lot when I am particularly Anxious and Concerned about something. It helps me to get the words out better. Sometimes.)

'Hello, Mum! Wow, what a truly SCRUMPTIOUS and delicious Aroma of delightful PROPORTIONS,' I would say in a Bright and Breezy manner as I entered the kitchen.

And Mum would say,
'Thank you, Summer dear. I am Concocting a supper fit for a princess, because that is what you are to me, my sweetie-pie.'

And I would reply, 'Oh good, because I would simply Adore to sit and have a cosy chat with you while you are cooking. You see, I REQUIRE a spot of motherly and wise advice about my relationship with Honey . . .'

I was just putting my key in the lock and muttering my final sentences to myself when Mum opened the door at the same time as me and said, 'Ah, Summer! Just the person I wanted to see.'

Well, what a strange thing to say, I thought. I am, after all, her beloved youngest daughter, so of course I am just the person she wanted to see.

'Summer Holly Love,' she said, 'we have to talk about that hound of yours.'

And I thought, Isn't it strange how Great Minds Think Alike?

2
How to Make a Right Dog's Dinner

'Oh, right!' I said to Mum, using the Bright and Breezy manner I had been practising in my head. 'That's funny, cos I was just about to say the same thing.'

Then I realized Mum was looking at me in a Distinctly unhappy manner: her eyes were actually BLAZING and dazzling, she was breathing rather more deeply than is normally necessary in an everyday kind of situation, and her nostrils were what I would describe as Scary and Flary.

'Oh?' said Mum, her eyebrows disappearing frighteningly fast into her fringe.

'Yeah,' I said, talking faster, hoping that my Brightness and Breeziness would soothe Mum's Scariness and Flariness. 'The thing is, I've been worried about Honey and how she isn't listening to me any more these days on the whole, and well I suppose I was kind of wondering if you and me – I mean, I – could sit down and have a cosy chat about it and figure out what I could do to – er – Progress Our Relationship To Another Level.'

(I'm not really sure where that last bit came from. It certainly hadn't been in the well-planned conversation in my head. 'Progress Our Relationship To Another Level' is the kind of thing they say in those serious Sunday-night-type dramas on the telly, which are basically boring love stories for grown-ups where everyone is miserable and not in love any more and they are trying to find a way to make up again. I only hope this doesn't happen with Nick and April as it looks like it's a right old palaver. I often think these people would be much happier if they just stopped weeping and moaning at each other and had a full-on WATER-FIGHT instead. It's much the best way to make friends with someone again when you have been arguing, I have found. Mainly because it's difficult to keep sulking when you are being sprayed with water and your friend is soaking wet and having a hysterical giggling fit. The other thing that always works is chocolate ice cream, but not for fighting with, of course.)

Water-fights and food? The perfect combination!

How to Make a Right Dog's Dinner

By this point Mum's nostrils had flared to such GINORMOUS proportions, I was worried that she might breathe in and suck me up into them. Urgh. I had to try really hard to concentrate on what she was saying instead of thinking about what the inside of her nostrils would be like.

'I think you've got more to worry about than "progressing your relationship", young lady,' Mum snarled.

I gulped.

Then I realized that Honey, who I'd thought was just sitting nicely at Mum's feet, was actually being held rather tightly by the collar and was not looking very happy about it.

Gulp!

Honey was also looking a bit odd. She seemed to have brown and red stuff smeared

19

all around her mouth, and she smelled strangely meaty.

'Shall I tell you what this delightful MUTT has just done?' Mum asked. (There was that unpleasant word again.) Somehow, I didn't think Mum was going to wait for an answer from me, and I was right. 'I came home from work early, as I had – and still have, in fact – a thumping headache. I went into the kitchen to get some water from the fridge, and I found this . . . this . . . ANIMAL . . . this HELL-HOUND . . . with the ENTIRE contents of the fridge all over the floor, FILLING HER FACE!'

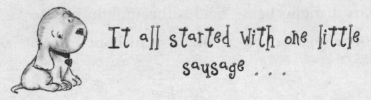

It all started with one little sausage . . .

It was at this Stage of the Proceedings that I noticed the state of the kitchen.

The fridge door was hanging open,

and milk cartons and yogurt pots and
those plasticky trays that sausages come in
were STREWN around the floor. It looked
as if the fridge had suffered an Almighty
EXPLOSION. I was actually hoping that
that really was the case, but then I looked at

Honey again, and it was obvious what had happened. She had eaten the lot. There was not one item of food left. Not a bean. Not a sausage. Not a single strand of anything. She had even eaten April's disgusting face-mask CONCOCTION that she insists on keeping in there – I could see the plastic tub she keeps it in, lying half-chewed on the floor next to an empty cheese wrapper. Now, that is what I call desperate. And I would have said so, only I was actually, really, truly speechless.

A TORRENT, as Molly would say, of questions raced through my head like the water bucketing over the Niagara Falls: How did Honey open the door? How did she even get into the kitchen, when I usually shut her in the back room before I leave for school? How did she even know to go to the fridge to find food – surely she couldn't have smelled it through the fridge door?

22

How to Make a Right Dog's Dinner

Slowly it Dawned Upon Me: I had been in a rush that morning. I had promised to meet Molly early so that we could catch up on our Celebrity Club, as we had missed out on a few meetings recently and we had some important dog-related celebrity stuff to discuss. Maybe I hadn't shut the door properly. And, actually, maybe I hadn't shut the fridge properly after getting my packed lunch out either.

Whoops. So it was *me* Honey had to thank for her mega-snack.

The pleasure was all mine!

'It's no good, Summer,' said Mum, sounding a bit calmer now that she could see how shocked I was. 'You are going to have to train this animal properly. First she chews shoes, then she helps herself to the Sunday roast, then she steals dishcloths and now . . . and now . . . THIS!'

She took a very deep breath and continued. 'You are going to clear up this mess, then we are going to ring Frank Gritter's mum and ask her where they went with Meatball to get her to behave so beautifully, and then you and Honey are going to obedience classes.'

I was totally and utterly MORTIFIED with an extra-large capital M – in other words, very upset. How could Mum stoop so low as to involve Frank Gritter in my life in any way? He was a boy and he smelt of socks. It would be Social Death at school if anyone realized that I was taking advice from Frank.

And as for obedience classes – that sounded far too much like extra school lessons to me.

I'm going to school? Yay!

3
How to Be One Girl and Her Dog

Have you ever noticed that life doesn't always go exactly how you have planned it? I seem to notice that more and more these days as I get more maturer. I know that I had been thinking that I needed to train Honey better, and I know that I had wanted to talk to Mum about it. But I certainly had not thought that her SOLUTION would involve Frank Gritter and extra lessons for me.

At least Mum didn't call Mrs Gritter straight away like she said she would. She had too much of a headache, I think, and anyway, it took me about five hours to clean up the mess Honey had made with all the packaging and eggshells and things she had left on the kitchen floor after her monster binge-out session in the fridge. By the time I had finished, Mum was flat out on her bed with a wet flannel on her forehead and the curtains drawn.

I decided it was the best place to leave her, so I went and quietly

did my homework and tried hard not to think about obedience classes. I thought that Molly would be frankly as APPALLED as me – in other words, horrified at the whole idea, and decided to chat to her about it as soon as I could.

The next day I asked Molly round after school so that we could talk in private. I didn't want Frank Gritter getting The Wind of anything before Mum had even called *his* mum. That would be far too embarrassing. So Molly and I had tea in the garden because the weather was quite nice and sunny, and I told her how Outraged I was at being sent to special dog classes.

I was expecting Molly to immediately tell me a Masterly Plan for how I could get out of this situation, but she totally flabbergasted me by having quite a different point of view.

'You keep saying you want to "bond with

Honey",' she reminded me. 'Well, obedience classes will be just the thing to "progress your relationship to another level".'

I made a humpfing noise and stared at my tuna sandwich. I had a Distinct Impression that Molly was laughing at me for some unknown reason, but I did not want to waste time trying to unfathom it at this PRECISE moment.

'Listen,' Molly said, in a tone of voice that sounded suspiciously like Mum when she's telling me something For My Own Good, 'these classes are exactly the kind of thing Monica Sitstill recommends dog owners to go to in her brilliant TV programme, *Love Me,*

28

Love My Dog. It'll be nothing like doing school-work, because we'll get to play games with Honey and meet loads of other like-minded owners and their dogs. It'll be like the puppy party we went to at the vets' when Honey was tiny!'

I made what Molly calls my Dubious Face when she said this, which is when I pull the corners of my mouth down and raise my eyebrows to show that I am not sure about something. I was Dubious about Molly thinking the puppy party had been fun, as all I could remember about it was that my annoying older sister, April, had come along and used the opportunity to make Nick Harris notice her, and Honey had hated him because of his beard, and I had hit my head and fainted.

 Those were the days!

But Molly was now Warming to Her Theme
– which means that she was getting really
very excited about the whole idea. Usually
when Molly gets excited I end up being
Infected by her Enthusiasm. (This does not
mean that I get a horrible disease from her,
or that a scab on my knee goes all pustular
or anything. It means that she gets so keen on
an idea that I end up getting excited about
it too.) But today I was finding it a bit more
difficult than usual to get Infected in this
way. I just frowned, while Molly got more
and more enthusiastical and talked on and on
about what *she* would be doing to get Honey
to behave like a highly trained and super-
obedient pooch.

'It'll be so cool!' Molly was saying.
Ignoring my Still-Dubious Face, she leaped up
and did a cartwheel, which made the cherry
tomatoes roll all over the picnic rug. Honey

tried to pinch one, and then remembered that she didn't actually like raw tomatoes.

Urgh! Horrid little
pippy things . . .

'I'll learn so much about how to train dogs that I'll be able to teach Honey to do tricks like they do AT CRUFTS!' she went on, her voice getting quite shrieky and, I must say, a little bit irritating. 'And then I, er I mean *we*,' she added hastily, finally catching sight of my Still-Still-Dubious Face, 'can enter competitions and win PRIZES. And then Honey'll be famous and will sit on one of those platforms that winning dogs sit on and she'll get a medal!' Unfortunately as she said this last bit she punched the air with her fist in a Symbol of Triumph — and whacked me in the face.

31

Her plans for future Fame and Fortune were then brought to a swift and sudden CLOSURE by the amount of blood gushing out of my nose. I ran into

the kitchen screaming while Honey jumped up and tried to lick my face. Gross.

Everyone's running around — I want to play too!

Mum cleared up the blood and put a packet of frozen peas on my nose (which was supposed to stop the swelling, but in actual fact just made my nose freeze so that I couldn't feel it any more), while Molly apologized over and over again.

Then the doorbell rang and it was Mrs
Cook, who said she was sorry but Molly
could not stay any longer at my house as she
had to go to her ballet class, which she had
obviously forgotten about in the excitement
of taking over my life. Personally I could not
have Given a MONKEY'S BANANA

MILKSHAKE that she had
to go early – in other words
I could not care less. I had
already had quite enough of
Molly's Infectious Enthusiasm for one day, plus
I was sure that my nose was swelling
up to the size of a small house at this
point and that I would look like a loop-the-loop
at school the next day.

Mrs Cook looked at me worriedly as she
left and said, 'You put your feet up, Summer.'

Quite why you need to put your *feet* up
when it is your *nose* that is hurting, I have no

idea. But I couldn't actually Physically say anything, as the pea packet was covering half my face, so now my mouth had started to freeze too.

Once Molly had gone I asked Mum, in a numb-mouthed kind of way, if she would help me go on to the Internet to look up about obedience classes in our area. Molly had really irritated me by taking over the whole idea of how I should Progress My Relationship with Honey and I decided that it would be better to get One Step Ahead of the Game and find out about training for myself. It had been bad enough when April had pretended Honey was her dog so that she could get a date with Nick. I was not going to let anyone else take away my puppy ever again.

Mum smiled. 'It's nice to see you taking a bit of initiative, Summer,' she said.

Actually I did have one more reason for

wanting to find out about classes on my own. And it didn't have anything to do with Molly. It was because I had no Desire in the faintest to let Mum call Frank Gritter's mum about it. Frank is such a Know-It-All annoying boy, and he would only have been full of RELISH at the fact that I was asking his mum for help.

I soon discovered that there were obedience classes at the local leisure centre. I knew the place well – there was a pool there called a leisure pool, which I used to love swimming in when I was smaller as it has a wave machine. I started to feel confident that I could cope with the obedience classes if they were in a place that I knew and that maybe Honey and I could go Just the Two of Us.

I scrolled down the screen and read a bit about the classes. They were run by a lady called Mrs Beatrice Woodshed, which sounded like rather a posh name, but there was no

35

photo of her, so I didn't know if she really was posh or not. I read on about when the classes were and what to bring with you (apart from your dog, of course) and I started to get really thrilled about the idea of what I would be able to teach Honey to do. Then I read a bit at the end of the website which cheered me up even more IMMENSELY:

http://www.leisurecentre457.com/train_that_dog

The course is run with the aim of enhancing the relationship between dog and owner. A dog learns fastest if he works consistently with only ONE master. We would therefore strongly discourage owners from bringing friends or family members with them to the classes as this merely distracts the dogs and makes our job harder.

How to Be One Girl and Her Dog

I wasn't sure what 'consistently' meant, but
I quickly realized that the website was being
Crystal Clear about one thing: Molly was not
going to be allowed to come with us. This
is what she herself would call an Interesting
Development – in other words, it was
completely unexpected. It was also really quite
helpful, as I now had a way of saying Kindly
But Firmly to Molly that she could not come to
the classes with me and Honey.

It would just be me and my pup – the
perfect team!

You said it!

4
How to End Up in the Dog House

Even though I was pleased that I had a reason to go to the classes without Molly, I must admit that I was more than a teensy-weensy bit worried about telling her. Still, I had a couple of days to work out how to say the exact words as the new session of classes didn't start till the beginning of the next week. I decided that Something Would Come To Me by then and that I should stop worrying about it for the moment.

So, This Was It! My pooch and I were

going to finally get the chance to work
together As One Being! It would be so cool
to teach Honey how to come and how to
stay and possibly then how to do tricks like
'sit up and beg' and 'roll over' and other truly
IMPRESSIVE stuff. Actually, the more I thought
about it, the more I realized that Honey would
probably become a SU*p*ERST*A*R.

I decided to tell her so.

'Honey, you will be the most obedient
pooch in the entire class and wow everyone
with your wonderous obedience!' I whispered,
tickling her soft, golden tummy.

 I'll do anything for a
Tummy-Tickle!

Yes, I, Summer Holly Love, would learn to be
truly Bonded as a pair with my dog and go on
to learn how to do those agility-type tricks and

39

probably one day win that most famous of all
dog shows, Crufts, just like Molly had said.

I soon ended up thinking that I could
Convince Molly to understand after all,
especially if I used the word 'consistent' in my
explanation. 'Consistent' was a Convincing
type of word, I thought. Also, Molly was my
most favouritest Best Friend, after all. She
was the only person in the world who had
ever been able to read my mind, plus she was
the only person who really understood my
Relationship with Honey. So of *course* she would
see how important it was for Honey to only
concentrate on one trainer, that is, me.

'Yes, I will be your Sole and Only trainer,
Honey Love,' I told my pooch.

Left a Bit, right a Bit
. . . aaah!

How to End Up in the Dog House

Just then Mum came to find me and said, 'Have you got Frank Gritter's number?'

'No!' I said. My heart sank down into the floor beneath me. I thought Mum had forgotten about calling the Gritters. We didn't need them now that we knew all about the classes.

And anyway, why on earth would Mum think that I would keep the number of a boy who PERMANENTLY stinks of socks? I know I should be nice about Frank because if it wasn't for him I wouldn't have Honey. And I *did* have his number when his dog Meatball had just had puppies, because then he was useful to me. But he is not at all useful to me now. I'm afraid that when someone stinks that badly of socks, it doesn't matter if they are as cool and handsome as James Bond – the stench of sock-whiff will always be the first thing you notice. Anyway, James Bond would never have

41

smelly socks. He would get a butler or someone
in the Secret Services to wash them and
possibly iron them for him. Then I thought,
how could I even *think* about the ODIOUS
Frank Gritter and the super-cool James Bond in

the same sentence? They are about as unsimilar as a baboon and, er . . . well . . . James Bond himself.

When Mum left, I got annoyed that Frank Gritter had gone like a worm into my thoughts again when I had been having a lovely time tickling Honey's tummy and dreaming about winning Crufts. Plus, I had found that whenever Frank popped into my thoughts (which I should point out is *not* at all often) he has a habit of appearing and annoying me. Like he did the next day.

I was in the playground, sitting on my favourite bench with Molly, and we were having one of our deep and intelligent chats about what had happened in the last episode of *Love Me, Love My Dog*, where a naughty spaniel had been trained not to jump up and STEAL SAUSAGES from the kitchen surfaces, and I was getting all excited and fluttery inside thinking what it is possible to teach your dog to do. Then smelly sock-stencher Frank Gritter butted in like he always does and HOLLERED at me:

'Mum says you're going to those obedience classes at the leisure centre. Apparently your mum asked if I would go with you and take Meatball to keep Honey company. Can't wait – I'd love to see someone teach *you* to be obedient, Summer Love! HAHAHAHAHA!'

He is so unfunny he makes my teeth go on their edges with fury. But I know he likes to wind me up and see me explode with anger so I clenched my teeth to stop them going on their edges and flashed him a fake smile and said in my most CONDESCENDING manner, 'Frank Gritter, I think you will find that obedience classes are for *dogs*, not mature and intelligent *girls*. You really should not poke your vast nose

44

in where it is not wanted. And talking of noses, mine is beginning to objectify to your appalling sock stench, so will you please remove yourself to the furthest corner of the playground.'

'OOOOOOOH!' was the only thing Frank could think of saying in return, which goes to show that the old wives' tale that boys are infinitely less maturer and generally more stupider than girls is absolutely one hundred and ten per cent correct, as if I didn't know that anyway by Natural Instinct.

I sat there with Molly on the bench and we just raised our eyebrows at one another and started talking about how bitten our nails were, which is our secret code for 'Changing the Subject so that the Enemy gets Bored and LEAVES US ALONE'.

Frank rolled his eyes and sneered and turned to one of his smelly footy mates and yelled a boy-sound along the lines of 'Awigh,

45

mate? Owsitgoin?' before launching a football at his friend's head.

This is apparently how boys say hello to each other.

'Phew, I can breathe again,' said Molly taking huge dramatical gulps of air now that *Mr Sewer Rat* had gone. 'Hey, it's great about  the obedience classes – we'll have to find a way of getting rid of Frank though . . . So, what time do we have to be there?'

I must have made a bit of an uncertain face at this point because I had been rather thrown by Frank bringing up the subject from deep Out Of The Blue like that, and I suddenly felt panicky about telling Molly she couldn't come with me.

I tried to bring the subject around to training being all about ONE girl and her dog. 'Did you know, I discovered something very interesting on the obedience class website and it is this: one dog cannot have two masters. Isn't that fascinating?'

Molly did not seem to get the hint that was CONCEALED so carefully in my comment and she said, 'Ah, but it can have two *mistresses!*' and looked very pleased with herself.

I tried again, 'Of course, it can be quite difficult to be consistentical when you have two mistresses . . .'

This had a bit more of an effect.

Molly narrowed her eyes and said, 'Are you saying that you don't want me to come with you?'

I had not expected such a direct response to my cunning and SUBTLE hinting and was a bit confused.

'Er – no – no, of course I want you to come!' I said.

(Fiddlesticks! I had not meant to say that.)

47

'Good, that's settled then,' said Molly. 'So when do the classes start?'

'Oh, er, I haven't a clue. I haven't enrolled or anything yet,' I said quickly, suddenly having a brilliant idea. 'In fact, I bet there are no spaces left. Actually, I kind of hope there aren't as I don't want to go with Frank Stinky-Features Gritter – do you?'

Molly smiled. 'You've got a point there, kiddo,' she said in her fake American accent that she uses when she's feeling CHIR*p*Y. (It can be a bit annoying when she does her fake American accent, but in the Circumstances I decided not to be annoyed this time: at least she wasn't narrowing her eyes at me any more.) 'But don't worry about Frank. I'm sure we can lose him somehow. It'll be OK – trust me,' she said in her normal voice.

I smiled back, but I was only smiling with

my mouth; it wasn't an all-over-body smile such as a true Best Friend should give if she *really* wants her friend to come with her to obedience classes.

'Yeah, you're right,' I agreed. 'It'll be OK.'

When did Life Get so Complicated?

Personally I blame it all on Frank Gritter.

5

How to Get into Another Fine Mess

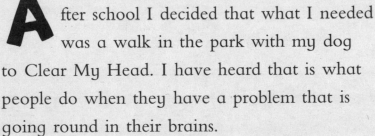

After school I decided that what I needed was a walk in the park with my dog to Clear My Head. I have heard that is what people do when they have a problem that is going round in their brains.

'Walkies' is always the answer.

April and Nick had been spending the day together, so when I got home to fetch Honey,

they said they would come to
the park with me. I personally
bet it was because Mum had asked them to.
She is not that keen on me going anywhere on
my own, even though I tell her that I am not
on my own; I am with Honey.

Anyway, we all arrived at the park and
headed in the direction of the doggy bit where
dogs are allowed off the lead.

The Best Bit.

That is to say, Honey and *I* headed in the
direction of the doggy bit. April was so busy
doing a nauseating hair-flicking display for
Nick's benefit that it's a miracle she could
even *see* where she was going. Honestly, if the
Olympics had a section for hair-flicking, April
would win it hands down (or should I say
'hands up', as her hands are usually FLAILING

51

in the air while she is
doing it). At any rate,
Honey and I decided
to leave her to
it and quickly
overtook her and
Nick. Luckily
they were talking
in low voices so that
I couldn't hear their
totally unfascinating
conversation, and then they
started kissing. I knew this because I could
hear the awful squelchy sound of their lips. It
makes me truly SHUDDER to remember it.
And as if all this wasn't bad enough, April was
also doing her 'Oh, please stop telling me I'm
so perfect' giggle, which is the most irritating
and sick-making noise in the whole of the
universe – after the sound of Frank Gritter

SｐEAKING ｔHROﾚGH BURｐS, of course.

You wouldn't *believe* the monstrous nature of this boy's burping ability. He can actually sing the whole of 'All Things Bright and Beautiful' in burps. And he is under the impression that this makes him some kind of a legend. What can I say? I will never understand boys. How April can have fallen in love with one, even if he is a grown-up, I will never know. I am sure Nick also sings in burps in private too. I am in fact positive that boys never grow out of this kind of DERANGED sense of humour.

So there they were, kissing and whispering, and there I was, walking very fast in front of them so that I could DEMONSTRATE clearly to the World At Large that I was nothing whatsoever to do with this slobbery couple.

Suddenly Honey yanked the lead out of my

53

hand, before I could let her off it myself, and hurtled HARUM-SCARUM in the direction of the little woody-type area for dogs.

Heaven!

(I like the word 'harum-scarum'. It is the only word to use to describe Honey's behaviour at that time. She did everything in a harum-scarum manner, given half a chance. Even coming to say hello was done like this, with her tail thrashing around in all directions, not even just side to side or up and down, but round and round in circles like a propeller. It quite baffled me where she found the energy. But then, eating the entire contents of the fridge on top of her daily dog dinners might have had something to do with it, I suppose.)

As I was at the End of my Wits with all

the lead-pulling business, and not in the mood
for being yanked into the air like a cartoon
person, I just let her go.

Watch out, everyBody! Here
I come . . .

I had come to the park to Get things Out Of
My System, after all, and it should be obvious
to anyone that you cannot do that if you
are being dragged along by a MAD AND
DERANGED dog.

However, I quickly realized that Honey
was Up to No Good. She was rolling in
something. And a dog rolling in something is
never a good sign.

Oh yes it is!

'Honey!' I cried. 'Come back! Honeeeeey!'

But, as usual, she was not listening at all. I shot a FURTIVE glance in the direction of my sister and Nick. Their faces were too close together for them to notice that anything had happened. In fact, they couldn't possibly have seen anything other than each other's eyeballs and noses.

'April! Honey's run off! I'm going after her!' I shouted and, not waiting for an answer, I hared over to the woody-type area.

It was as I had feared. Honey was in doggy heaven – that is, she was rolling in poo.

This is a good one!

'Phew! What a stench!' I cried.

I tried to get hold of Honey's collar to pull her away, but she was not in a frame of mood to let me.

No way.

Plus, I was desperately trying not to touch any place on her fur which had come into contact with the poos. I sort of danced around her, looking for a poo-free patch of fur, and then pounced.

'Aeeeeeeeeeeeeeei!' I yelled, as Honey leaped up and licked me all over. Needless to say, this did not help with my Poo-Avoidance Plan.

I like to spread a bit of happiness.

'Summer! Are you all right?' Nick had managed to DETACH himself from my sister's face long enough to notice that I was not walking in front of them any more. But it seemed he was not intelligent enough to

57

notice that I was anything BUT 'all right'.
(Honestly, I thought you had to be clever and
PERCEPTIVE to be a vet.)

'NOOOOOOOOOOOO!' I howled. 'I am
not ALL RIGHT! I am covered in poos that
are stenching their way to the high heavens!'

I'm embarrassed to have to admit that I
was actually blubbing at this point. It was not
a clever reaction to the state of affairs, as it
meant the tears were mixing in with all the
muck I had on me. Not the sort of attractive
look that would get me
through the finals of the TV
talent show *Seeing Stars*, I
shouldn't think.

Nick grabbed Honey by the collar and
said, 'No!' firmly.

 WHY? WHAT? WHERE?

How to Get into Another Fine Mess

Then he grabbed me by the hand and said,
'Let's get you home,' but not so firmly. April
crossed her arms, flicked her hair and curled her
lip. I knew that could only mean one thing.
Trouble.

When we got home Nick offered to hose
Honey down for me, but April gave him such
a look that he ended up saying goodbye rather
hastily and left without even kissing her. April
didn't even object, which I thought at the time
was rather un-girlfriend-like, but actually, when
you think about it, I don't think I would want
to let someone who has touched the collar of a
poo-stained dog and the hand of a poo-stained
girl kiss me goodbye anyway. Even if I liked
kissing. Which I don't.

April flounced off to her room and I
cringed. Flouncing is not a Good Sign. It
generally means there will be Words later

59

on, most probably when Mum is around to WITNESS them. Anyway, part of me was rather relieved she had flounced instead of starting a shouting match, which is another thing she does when she claims I have done something to upset her.

As I was on my own, I decided that I would take the Initiative and hose Honey down before Mum got home. Mum had made it quite plain that she was not interested in cleaning up any more of Honey's messes. In fact, only the other day she had said in a rather careless and frankly uncaring tone:

'*You* wanted a dog, Summer, so *you* have to put up with all that goes with being a dog owner.'

'Even the poo?' I had cried, in an outraged and wounded manner.

'*Especially* the poo,' she had replied firmly. And the subject was then well and truly closed.

60

How to Get into Another Fine Mess

She is so unfeeling and not at all sympathetic, which is not what you expect from a mum at all.

Anyway, after this conversation I looked in my very own copy of my very favourite book, *Love Me, Love My Dog* (which is based on the fabulous TV show of the same name), and I discovered a truly astounding fact:

> Often ordinary dog shampoos are not powerful enough to combat the pungency of certain odours, notably that of fox's faeces.

I had never seen the word 'faeces' before. At first I had read it as 'faces'. I had thought, What on earth is so smelly about a fox's face? Then I had looked at the word again and realized it had two 'e's in it. I often read things wrong. (Mr Elgin, our teacher, says it is because I am 'Careless and Slapdash' which is quite unfair, I must say, because I always try

my hardest in English, as it is a subject that
I like. Unlike history, which does not teach a
person anything that can ever be of any use
to their practical life whatsoever.) Anyway, I
had to look up 'faeces' in the dictionary, and
I was amazed to see that it is a *pOSH*
 **WORD FOR** *poo!* Imagine the word
'poo' having a posh name! What
will they think of next, I wonder?
So once I knew that Monica
Sitstill was talking about fox poo, I had to
read on:

> The advice I was given by another
> dog trainer was to smother the dog
> in tomato ketchup before hosing him
> down.

This woman has some very
Interesting and Alternative Ideas, I
thought to myself – in other words, she's stark

raving bonkers. But I couldn't help being impressed as I read on:

> The acid in the tomato ketchup neutralizes the odour.

Now that Honey and I actually were covered in real-life poo and I actually had a real-life Honk Fest to deal with, I thought it would be the perfect opportunity to try out the Wise and Wonderful Words of Monica Sitstill.

With her brilliant tips and hints to follow, I couldn't possibly fail to clean up this little mess, I thought to myself.

Could I?

63

6

How to Deal with a Honk Fest

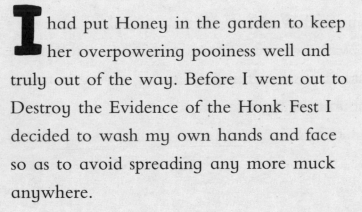

I had put Honey in the garden to keep her overpowering pooiness well and truly out of the way. Before I went out to Destroy the Evidence of the Honk Fest I decided to wash my own hands and face so as to avoid spreading any more muck anywhere.

Then I opened the fridge and had a good look for some ketchup – there was none. I also checked all the cupboards – no luck. Very odd indeed. We are never a No-Ketchup household.

How to Deal with a Honk Fest

Then I remembered that Mum had said  she was going to the supermarket on the way back from work.

'Aha!' I thought. 'She will be on a ketchup-restocking mission.'

But then my face fell. I could not wait until Mum came home before I washed Honey. The poo would by then be completely ENCRUSTED on her fur and would be even tougher than ever to wash off, and she would have to be officially renamed as Miss Honksville, Arizona, 2008.

'Right,' I said to myself. 'What would Molly do in a situation like this? She would say that I must think LATERALLY.' Which would be her way of saying, 'What else could you use instead of ketchup?'

I had a sudden FLASH of inspirationalism. It was such a bright flash that I almost fell over at my own brilliance.

'What is tomato ketchup made of?' I asked myself in a RHETORICAL manner – which means that I was not expecting a reply from anyone as I was on my own. 'Tomatoes!' I answered myself. 'I'm sure Monica Sitsill didn't mean it had to be *actual* ketchup – maybe another kind of tomato sauce would do the trick.'

I started to scan the shelves of the cupboard for other types of tomato sauce. Mum usually has loads of jars because we all love pasta in this family – especially lasagne, but that's another story . . .

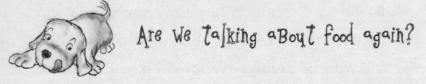

Are we talking about food again?

I shuffled all the bottles and jars around until I spotted a familiar orangey label on a large jar of distinctly tomatoey Italian pasta sauce:

How to Deal with a Honk Fest

'Aha! Tomaaaatoes! Beeeeuuuuutiful tomaaaaatoes!' I shouted in an over-the-top Italian accent, because I was so relieved to have found it, and also because I knew no one was listening.

Pulling on a pair of rubber gloves that Mum uses for housework, I went out into the garden.

I called Honey to me and held out a treat in my hand to get her to come, which she did very eagerly.

All I have to do is say hello and I get a treat!

Then I quickly tipped the whole jar of sauce over her neck which is where most of the poo had been rubbed in. Then, while Honey was still chewing her treat, I leaped over her so that I had one leg on either side to stop her from

running off, and I started to rub the sauce into
her golden fur.

'This is a very odd thing to do to a dog,'
I said to myself, but I did think I could smell
more tomatoey odours than pooey ones, which
could only be a Good Thing.

Honey unfortunately quite liked the smell
of the sauce too, and kept trying to twist round
and lick it off, but I had already managed

to get the Advantage with the Element of Surprise. (Well, *I'd* be surprised if someone up-ended a jar of sauce over me.)

Time to wash it off, I thought eventually and went to get the hose.

Unfortunately, Honey took one look at the hose and decided that she didn't fancy a wash.

Keep that snake away from me.

She then went into a particularly over-the-top harum-scarum kind of mood and ran around the garden in the manner that Molly would describe as Headless Chicken Mode. (Not a great description, I always think, as how on earth can an animal or bird run around when it's had its head chopped off? I know that if

I had my head chopped off, I would drop down dead. Or maybe I wouldn't. I suppose I wouldn't be alive to find out. Anyway, I have no INTENTION of letting anyone chop my head off just to see whether I run around in a demented and deranged way, so there's no point in dwelling on it.)

By this time, I was quite covered in tomato sauce myself and beginning to wonder if Monica Sitstill had any idea that this would really work in true life, or if in fact it was some kind of horrid joke she had written to see if anyone would actually be daft enough to try it.

Then I thought I really ought to just get on and finish off the Job In Hand, which was of course to wash the sauce off Honey.

As is usual with new ideas and things, this was Easier Said Than Done.

I chased Honey all around the garden squirting her with the hose. In the end I had to

stop because I was out of breath. And anyway,
I thought I had done a pretty good job of
cleaning off the sauce. Honey rolled over and
over in the grass to dry herself.

Rolling does it for me.

I wondered if it had worked: was Honey still
a stinkified pooch of pooey persuasion, or a
heavenly scented hound?

When I walked into the kitchen to get a
towel to finish drying her, I found Mum was
back. She was frantically searching through
the fridge and the cupboards and muttering to
herself.

'Where is that sauce? I wasn't supposed to
buy sauce. I know we *had* sauce. How am I
supposed to make pasta and sauce for tea if
there is no sauce?'

Whoops.

'Mum . . .'

'Oh, Summer. Do you know where the
– what in the name of . . . WHAT have you
got all over your T-shirt?' Mum sort of shrieked
the last bit, which made me jump back
like I imagine A STARTLED
RABBIT might do if a dog
barked at it.

My mind was ticking over at probably
two hundred kilometres a minute. It must have
been at least that much, because my head was
actually spinning. I was desperately trying to
think up a way of explaining about the poo
and the tomato sauce and Monica Sitstill's
brilliant tips and hints, in a manner that would
stop Mum from exploding.

'Mum, you'll never believe this—' I started
speaking but was stopped by a furry whirlwind
of golden and, er . . . pink that came hurtling
through the door and knocked me flying before

jumping up to lick Mum's angry face.

Hi, there! Missed me?

'Summer,' said Mum, in a dangerously quiet and low tone of voice which usually means you-are-in-so-much-trouble-you-have-no-idea-how-much.

I froze in horror, which was quite difficult in my crumpled position on the kitchen floor.

'Summer Holly Love,' Mum continued, 'would you like to explain to me why you and your mutt are covered in tomato sauce?'

It was then that I got a good look at Honey – something which had not been possible while she had been careering around the garden, rolling in the flower beds and rubbing her fur on the grass.

What I saw made me stare.

73

My mouth hung open and I think I stopped breathing. I forgot how to speak and I had to pinch myself to make sure that I was in fact seeing with my own eyes and not through the eyes of a dreaming person.

Honey's fur had turned pink.

And it had CHUNKS oF oNIoN in it.

She was a walking advert for the Italian tomato-sauce-making people.

 Don't I look pretty in pink?

74

7

How to Behave (Dis-)Obediently

The day of the first obedience class dawned.

That was supposed to sound poetical, but it doesn't, because, let's face it, there is nothing very poetical about the word 'obedience', even if you put it near the word 'dawned'.

And there was certainly nothing poetical about the day after the tomato sauce INCIDENT either. Mum had been so furiously beside herself with anger that there was NO WAY HO-ZAY that I was going to get out of

going to the classes with Frank and Meatball.
So that was that. I had to go to the class with
a stinky boy that I didn't want to be with.
And I couldn't even tell my best friend about
it, because she wasn't supposed to know about
it. Oh, and Honey's fur was still as pink as a
poodle's after a session in a pamper
parlour (except there were still bits
of onion in it too, and I don't suppose
you get them in pooches' pamper
parlours − or any other kind of pamper parlour,
come to that).

I didn't think things could get any worse . . .

The minute we arrived at the leisure centre,
Honey spotted Meatball through the car
window and got very excited indeed. She
started jumping up and down and barking and
licking the window and spreading her dog snot
all over it.

76

Hey, Mum! It's me – Your darling daughter!

Mum hates it when Honey smears her dog snot all over the windows. I don't understand why she has to make such a fuss about it: it's not as if our car would have won any prizes for Cleanest and Sprucest Car of the Year Award *before* we got a dog. There have always been crumbs and grains of sand and muddy stains everywhere. (Although the snot is a relatively new addition to the MAYHEM, it is true.)

'Hi, Summer!' Frank shouted as I got out of the car and let Honey out of the boot. Then he saw her New Look and guffawed: 'Holy Christmas Crackers, mate! What's happened to your hound? Has she had a girly makeover or something? Boy, does she look *mega* weird.'

Thanks, Frank, I thought. As if it wasn't

humiliating enough to be seen in public with a pink Labrador, I now had to put up with having it BROADCAST in a highly embarrassing way across the whole car park.

But I decided that as Ignorance is Bliss, I should ignore him and say nothing. So I put all my efforts into concentrating on fixing Honey's lead so that she didn't hurtle off and crash straight into Meatball, which was obviously what she was desperate to do.

'Summer,' Mum said irritably from the driver's seat, 'will you please hurry up – Frank's waiting for you.'

Which, of course, was precisely why I was not hurrying up. But there was a car behind ours now and the man who was driving it was beeping the horn and waving angrily, so finally I got the lead fixed and said, 'See you later, Mum. Come on, Honey.'

Honey immediately leaped on top of

How to Behave (Dis-)Obediently

Meatball and Meatball rolled over so that
Honey could have a good sniff, and I got
pulled on top of them both.

Why don't you join us?

'Ha-ha!' Frank laughed. He was still managing
to hold on to Meatball and not be pulled over,
which was distinctly annoying. 'I see what your
mum means!'

As I struggled to get up and pull Honey off Meatball I hissed, 'What is your point exactly?'

Frank smirked. 'Well, you obviously can't control your dog, or should I say your *furry flamingo*?'

I huffed and again ignored his most unhilarious comment. 'If *you* had more control over *your* dog, Frank Gritter, then you would not let her roll over and have her bottom sniffed by *my* dog.'

Frank shrugged and said, 'Whatever. Come on, let's go in.'

I was SEETHING with anger. Why on earth did I have to put up with this? According to Mum and Mrs Gritter, Meatball was so well behaved she didn't *need* these classes, so why was Frank even here?

We all walked in through some glass doors and made our way to the main hall, where the classes were being held.

How to Behave (Dis-)Obediently

As if reading my thoughts (which I jolly
well hope he can't in true life) Frank said, 'You
know I'm only here cos Mum said I had to
look after you.'

'I do NOT need "looking after"!' I said,
rather too loudly, and lots of people stared at
me. And then of course they all saw Honey
and probably thought that actually I very
much *did* need looking after.

Frank just smirked again.

There was a queue at the door to the hall.
I hate queuing, especially next to someone who
stinks. It's ridiculous how much grown-ups seem
to adore queuing. I think they would queue for
a queue given half of a chance.

Honey was pulling on the lead so hard that
I had to push my feet into the ground and lean

backwards to stop her from running off with
me in tow.

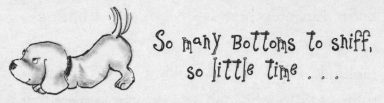

So many Bottoms to sniff,
so little time . . .

I also was trying desperately not to topple into
Frank, who would have made some horrid joke
about me 'falling into his arms' or something,
knowing him.

Eventually we got nearer the top of the
queue and I watched carefully while the owners
in front of me talked to a lady sitting at a
small table which was covered in bits of paper
and charts and things. Everyone was telling her
their names and handing over the money for
the classes and then the lady was explaining
that they needed to go and stand in a circle
around the edge of the hall.

Frank and I paid our money and went to

join the circle. In the middle was one Scary
Mary of a lady.

'Oh my goodness dearie me,' I said to
myself. 'She is EXCEPTIONALLY bizarre-
looking.'

Uh-oh! That woman looks
fierce . . .

I knew it was most probably an unkind and
quite Uncharitable Thing to think, but this
woman looked really quite bag-ladyish. I
mean, you would have thought she could at
least have put a brush through her grey tangly
hair and found a few clothes that matched.
It certainly didn't give me a very good First
Impression. (We are always told by adults that
First Impressions Count.)

I, in fact, had made quite a big effort to
make sure that my First Impressions did Count,

if I do say so myself. I was wearing my most smartest denim miniskirt with pink hearts sewn on and my T-shirt was pink and had a large purple heart on it. So you see I had thought about how to coordinate myself, heart-wise. I had even managed to tie back my hair (which is mostly best described as UNRULY) into a purple scrunchy. (I am trying to grow it, but it's quite depressing, as curly hair doesn't seem to grow downwards, only outwards. My real ambition is to have long blonde hair like April has. Although I would never tell her that, as it would make her even more UNBEARABLE if she knew I wanted to look anything like her. I thought that if I grew mine, I could get hold of some of those straightener thingies and maybe persuade Molly to help me bleach it. It does sound a bit desperate, I know, but Desperate Times Call For Desperate Measures, as they say. And all the people on *Seeing Stars* seem to have long blond hair that is straight. Even the men.)

Frank, of course, was *not* looking as if he even knew what a First Impression was, unless he thought it meant 'Look as smelly and gross as you can so that no one will want to stand anywhere near you.'

That boy smells just SWEET to me!

This woman, whom I had realized by now must be Mrs Beatrice Woodshed, was talking to some of the other dog owners in a growly low voice that sounded like a man's. Actually, the closer I inspected her, the more I started to wonder if she *was* in fact a man. Perhaps she was one of those men you get in pantomimes who always play the Dames by squeezing into dresses and smearing on lipstick and calling

85

themselves Old Mother
Marjory (or in this case,
'Beatrice'). Or
I supposed it
was just about
FEASIBLE that
she could have
been a very ugly
woman in true real
life. In any case,
she was called *Mrs*
Woodshed, not Old
Mother Woodshed,
and she didn't
say anything
pantomimical like 'Oh, no it isn't' or 'He's
behind you', and she was wearing a normal-ish
skirt rather than a pantomime one. (Actually
it was a bit like a tartan sack. It was also as
wide as it was long and sat very high up on

her body, sort of just under her — how can I put this? — well, her Bosom really. Which was what you might describe as Ample. But not in a good way.) And she had a kind of smear of red lipstick that was running out of the line of her lips in a *LEAKY* fashion. She also had alarming blue stuff on her eyelids. *But* she also had a small black moustache. And very hairy eyebrows. My knees were knocking already, and the class hadn't even started yet.

Blimey, I thought, if Honey didn't like beards, she sure wasn't going to like the sight of Mrs Bag Lady Woodshed. She was double-plus-mega scary with an extra layer of scariness; even Monica Sitstill would have quivered in her pointy leather boots at the sight of that Ample Bosom, I was sure.

However, Honey did not seem at all Fazed by Mrs Woodshed or her Bosom, or indeed any of the other dogs or dog owners, most of whom

87

were staring straight at me and my pink pooch in a most off-putting and rude fashion.

I forced myself not to look at them and also made a super-mega effort to drag my INCREDULOUS gaze away from Mrs Woodshed's Bosom, because she was now talking to all of us.

'Everyone!' she growled, above the noise of people chatting and dogs barking.

The dogs pricked up their ears and strained even harder on their leashes. Honey seemed to be the most excited of all the dogs in the room, which I feared did not bode well for the rest of the class.

The pongy whiffs! The waggy tails!

As it happened, my fearings about bodings proved to be correct.

Mrs Woodshed carried on. 'Today is the first class, so we are going to concentrate on the first and most important lesson that you need to teach your dog. And that is how to SIT on command—'

Well, how easy peasy is that? I smirked to myself.

Then Honey made a lunge for Meatball's bottom.

Come and play, Mum, per-leese!

'Excuse me! Will the owner of the PINK dog please exercise a little more control?' Mrs Woodshed roared as Honey crashed into her wide tartan skirt, dragging me after her.

'I thought that's what *you* were here to teach,' I muttered angrily as I went skidding across the slippery floor of the hall.

'Summer!' Now Frank was having a go at

me. As if he couldn't see that I was somewhat
busy trying to get my dog away from his dog.

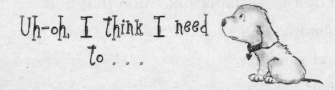

Uh-oh, I think I need
to . . .

'Summer!' He was shouting at me now, but
I was rather tied up with Honey in what
Molly would call a LITERAL manner – in
other words, I really was tied up in true life in
Honey's lead, with my feet sliding everywhere.

How to Behave (Dis-)Obediently

'That's strange,' I thought. 'Why *is* the floor so slippery? Honestly, I could break my—'
'PINK DOG OWNER!' Mrs Woodshed was yelling at me and her face was redder than mine ever goes. 'Will you just LOOK at what your puppy has done!'

I'm sorry. It was
an . . .

I realized that the room had gone quiet. No one was talking, not even Frank. Even the other dogs were no longer barking. I looked down at Honey who seemed to be the centre of attention. And no wonder.

. . . accident.

She had done a pee on the floor some way
behind us, and I had managed to drag her
through it, so now there was a line of pee
stretching the whole length of the sports hall.

I was quite possibly even more embarrassed
than the day I was acting as a mermaid in the
Christmas play in Year One and my tail fell
down and took my knickers with it.

So I stood there in the middle of the hall,
being shouted at, with Frank Gritter laughing
his head off, my pink puppy jumping up and
wagging her tail and being all cheery and
licky-faced and bouncy, my feet covered in
pee, and all I could think was:

'I wish Molly was here.'

8
How to Open Your Mouth and Put Your Foot in It

Of course, however much I wanted to, I *couldn't* talk to Molly about the completely disastrous tragedy that was the obedience class. I was desperate, in fact, to keep it all a secret, as I knew she would be very hurt and upset if she found out that I had gone without her, and even worse than that – that I had gone with Frank Gritter. Also, I had actually told her a Bare-Faced Lie of the kind my sister April would have been proud of, because I had actually said that I had not yet enrolled.

93

But she found out anyway.

We were lining up to go swimming and I was standing in a pair with Molly as usual, because she's my Best Friend and there is no one else in the whole world, or indeed the universe, that I would rather line up in a pair with, even when she's being bossy.

We were talking about our Celebrity Club and how we had loads to sort out, when along came Mister Stink-i-verse, A.K.A. (which Molly says means 'otherwise known as' but then shouldn't it be O.K.A?) Frank Gritter.

'So, did you tell your mum about Honey peeing everywhere last night?' he guffawed, right across the queue of everyone lining up for swimming. He was doing a lot of guffawing in my direction lately, and I was not sure I approved.

I turned my back on him and pretended that I had not heard a word. But I could tell

that my face had gone bright red in the most
clashing-with-my-hair kind of way.

'*What* did Honey do?' Molly asked, her
mouth hanging open in a very disbelieving
manner. 'And, er, why does Mr Putrefying
Sock Odour know about it and not me?' she
added, doing the narrow-eyed thing that
always flusters me.

'Sorry?' I said calmly, playing for time.

'You heard me,' said Molly impatiently.

'Oh, right, Honey. Yeah. She, er . . . Oh, I
can't say! It's just so gross,' I said lamely.

Gross? Me?

'Summer!' Molly snapped, making me jump.
She looked pretty fierce, and I got all confused
and didn't watch what I was saying next as
carefully as I should have done.

'She peed all over the floor, and I went and

95

dragged her through it without realizing and then everybody in the whole class laughed at me,' I said very quickly and then groaned.

'*Everybody?*' Molly said slowly. She looked like one of those scary policemen on telly when they are crossly-questioning burglars and other criminal types. Honestly, that girl has got a bright future ahead of her as a detective, I swear it. She says she wants to be a journalist and work on one of those celebrity magazines, but personally I think her talents of DEDUCTION and DETECTION would be wasted.

How to Open Your Mouth and Put Your Foot in It

'Er, yeah, everybody — as in, you know, Mum and April—' I began, realizing in a worried manner that I had really and truly given too much away and was in danger of getting stuck in troubled waters up to my neck and then probably drowning.

'Hang on just a minute, Summer Holly Love,' said Molly. Now she was sounding like Mum again. 'How come your mum and April were with you as well as "the whole class"? Did you have a party last night without me, or — oh no . . .' Molly stopped in mid-tracks and a look of horrified shock froze her face into a mask.

I took a deep breath and waited for the explosion . . .

'You went to the obedience class last night — *without me!*' she hissed.

. . . Bang.

At that moment our teacher told us off for

talking and we had to go and get changed for swimming.

Molly did not speak to me for the whole of that entire lesson. At first I thought that it wasn't that strange, as you can hardly chat to your friend when you are having to do front crawl with your face in the water. I spent the lesson thinking maybe Molly would be concentrating so hard on not drowning that she would forget about our conversation. After all, front crawl is a particularly tricky stroke to do and actually, come to think of it, has nothing whatsoever to do with crawling. I mean, you don't crawl along the bottom of the pool on your hands and knees like a baby. In fact you look more like a KILLER OCTOPUS charging after its victim in a stormy sea.

I was thinking about

this afterwards when I suddenly realized that
I was the only one left in the changing room.
Molly had not waited for me. It is actually
quite normal for me to be the last one left
getting changed, as I am quite a slow dresser.
('The slowest dresser in the West', April calls
me – as if *she* can talk! She takes about five
hours just to blow-dry her precious hair.) But
normally Molly hangs around and tells me to
hurry up or helps me to sort out my hair, which
seems to have even more of an AVERSION
to being brushed after spending half an hour
scrunched up inside a swimming hat.

I ran out of the changing rooms to find my
shoes and see where Molly had got to. But she
was already lining up to go back to class and
was in a pair with – oh no! Rosie Chubb!

Rosie Chubb is the most annoyingest of
the girls in our year. She talks all the time
in a most yawnsome manner, mostly about

99

her ballet class, which Molly says she has
the MISFORTUNE to do with her. (Molly
is faberoony at ballet, but doesn't go on and
on about it like Rosie, who is actually not
that TALENTED.) And she has a laugh like
a hyena who's just swallowed a squeaky
children's toy – in other words, screechy and
bonkers. She doesn't have any real friends, but
she has this Knack of spotting when someone
has had a Falling Out with their real friend,
and then she just goes in like a worm and
makes a bad situation even more worse by
taking sides.

I have told Mum all about this, but she is
not at all Sympathetic in the way that mums
should be about this kind of problem. She just
says, 'Poor Rosie. I expect *she* feels left out all
the time. She's only trying to get attention –
why don't you ask her round to play with you
and Molly some time?'

How to Open Your Mouth and Put Your Foot in It

Honestly, I sometimes wonder if Mum was
ever a girl with a best friend.

Anyway, I decided that I would be bold
and brave and walk straight up to them
and pretend that I hadn't noticed Rosie was
trying to steal my friend. I even felt a little bit
confident that Molly would not actually be
listening to Rosie because she is usually quite
rude about her.

'Thanks for waiting, Molly,' I said in an
ironical manner.

Molly and Rosie stopped chattering and just
stared at each other as if I wasn't there at all.

'Oh, Molly – did you just hear something?'
said Rosie in her squeaky voice.

'No, Rosie,' said Molly, doing an
impression of an over-the-top actor looking
around and being surprised. 'I didn't hear a
thing. Now, what were we just saying about
the *pas de deux*?'

101

'Molly—' I tried again, even though I knew my face had once again gone that awful hot deep-red colour I hate so much.

'Oh yes, the *PAS DE DEUX* . . .' Rosie started talking loudly over the top of me. 'We're doing it next ballet class, remember? You can be my partner, Molly.'

I was in a good mind to shove Rosie Chubb rather hardly in the back, but I caught our swimming teacher looking in our direction and decided I should be DIGNIFIED and walk away. I started walking to the back of the line and put all my effort into not letting any tears spill out over the edges of my eyes. I stared very straight and in a fixed way at the ground and

How to Open Your Mouth and Put Your Foot in It

fiddled around with my swimming bag a lot
so that anyone who was watching me would
think I was just busy and not upset at all.

I was staring at the ground so much that I
didn't notice who I had been paired up with to
walk back to school until a voice said:

'Hey, Summer! Looks like it's your lucky
day!'

Frank Gritter. Complete with slightly damp
smelly socks.

My lucky day indeed.

9

How to Put a Brave Face on Things

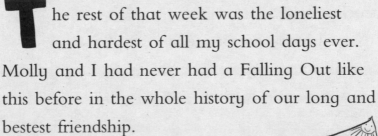

The rest of that week was the loneliest and hardest of all my school days ever. Molly and I had never had a Falling Out like this before in the whole history of our long and bestest friendship.

Every day Molly was crammed up next to Rosie on a different table from our usual one, and they were giggling and whispering together non-stop. A couple of

times I tried to catch Molly's eye, but she just looked away and started whispering again. I knew they were talking about me. To distract myself from this CALAMITY, I learned to keep my head down and drew doodly pictures of Honey on the cover of my notebook.

Honey was no longer a pink pooch, thank the high heavens, as the sauce had at last come off after a few more hose-related washing events. I tried to cheer myself up by thinking about how funny it was when I chased her with the hose and I even tried doodling a picture of that on the cover of my notebook too.

None of this stopped me from feeling sad though, and more than once drops of tears fell out of the edges of my eyelids and SPLASHED on to the doodly pictures. It made the ink run and was very annoying.

★

105

Pup Idol

Friday was a particularly bad day, as normally Fridays were my and Molly's best day of the week. We called them 'Mad Fridays' because we were always in a fabulous mood, giggling together and planning stuff for the weekend. But that Friday she didn't talk to me or look at me all day. It was more like 'Sad Friday'.

I dripped tears on to the pavement all the way home that afternoon, because I realized I was going to be having a very lonely weekend. When I got home I ran straight to Honey and buried my soggy face in her lovely clean fur. That made me feel much better.

What are friends for?

If Molly was going to pretend that I was not her best friend any more, then that was fine. Honey was my best friend really these days.

106

How to Put a Brave Face on Things

We were One Girl and Her Dog. A Team to
be Reckoned With.

I let Honey out into the garden and she
ran in crazy circles around the tree while I got
myself a cool drink and a snack. Then I gave
Honey a little dog treat to show her how much
I loved her and said, 'You're the best
dog in the world, Honey Love!'

These are the Best
TREATS in the World.

She did some more crazy circles after this,
while I read the note that Mum had left on the
kitchen table.

Hi Summer!
Hope you had a good day!

(Not really, Mum, but thanks for
asking . . .)

I'll be a bit late tonight —
but don't worry, I've made a
lasagne.
April said she'd babysit as
Nick's coming over, so you can
all eat together.

Babysit? *Babysit?* Did she even *know* how old
I was? Honestly, I sometimes wondered if she
had even *looked* at me recently.

I popped the lasagne in the
oven to heat it up and went to
see what was on telly later, as
I had no Intention whatsoever of sitting round
the table with April and Nick on a Friday
night, pretending to be happy to share their
company. Not to mention the lasagne.

Yeah, What's ours is ours . . .

As I flicked sadly and MOROSELY through the list of telly programmes in the newspaper I noticed something so fantastic that I almost forgot how glum I was feeling.

There was a new dog-lover type programme on that very night! It was called *Pup Idol* and this is what the paper said about it:

This new and exciting programme is *Crufts* meets *Seeing Stars* – a sure-fire hit for dog lovers everywhere. The highly entertaining show takes dogs from rescue homes and pairs them up with celebrities. The celebrities then learn to train their dogs to complete an agility course. The well-known trainer Monica Sitstill sits on a panel of judges who deliver their verdict on the performances, and the audience at home is invited to phone in and vote for the dog of their choice!

I almost stopped breathing. This was the most inspirationalist bit of telly programming I had ever heard of. It certainly was enough to stop me thinking, for a little while at least, about Molly and Frank Gritter and obedience classes and all the other things that had ruined my life recently.

Even though it was Friday night and I had the whole weekend to do it, I decided to do my English homework to Get It Out of the Way. It was on Astounding and Amazing Alliteration and was quite exceptionally easy. Then I got my tea ready quickly so I could eat it in front of the faberoony new programme.

Eventually I was serving up my lasagne, ready to settle down with my wonderful dog, when I heard one of the sounds that is guaranteed to make my brain fizz up with annoyance: my sister's tinkly laugh, used only for the benefit of Mr Nick Harris. Sure enough,

How to Put a Brave Face on Things

I then heard the sound of Mr Nick Harris's chuckle, which I am sure *he* uses only for the benefit of Miss April Lydia Love.

I decided to dash into the sitting room and pounce on the sofa to grab the best telly-watching spot before they got there and started snogging again.

'Watch out!' shouted April as Honey and I hurtled harum-scarum-like past them, me clutching my supper and Honey sticking to me like the Girl's Best Friend that she is.

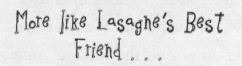 

More like Lasagne's Best Friend . . .

'Hello, Summer,' said Nick. 'How's Honey? No more incidents involving nasty smells, I hope?'

'No, she's fine, thanks,' I replied. I avoided eye contact as I didn't want to give up my place on the sofa and risk missing a single second of the new show. Nor did I wish to witness another Session of Slurpy Snogging (I wonder what Mr Elgin would think of that fine example of alliteration?), which would frankly have put me off my lasagne.

Not a problem – I'd polish it off!

April huffed loudly and made some comment about not watching 'a load of old rubbish with her baby sister', but I wasn't really listening.

Honey came and sat by my feet as I got comfy with my lasagne and the remote control. She was being so cute and loving in my Hour of Need.

Hey, this is MY Hour of Need, actually . . .

How to Put a Brave Face on Things

There were a few adverts, and then *Pup Idol* started, with the marvellous Monica Sitstill introducing the show! She was looking as scary and impressive as ever, wearing a short leather skirt and extra-pointy high-heeled boots that went up to her knees. 'Not very practical for dog-training,' I said to myself; but then I remembered she was only being a judge on this show and not actually doing any of the training, so she was allowed to be Glam.

'I was delighted when I was asked to help make this show,' she was saying. 'Agility is a wonderful way to bond with your dog. Dogs love to learn new things, and really there is no truth in the saying, "You can't teach an old dog new tricks" – you can! Every minute you spend with your dog teaching him new things is a minute well spent.'

At this I sat up and paid a lot more attention. This was the kind of advice I had been looking for! I was so fixated to the screen that I had forgotten about the lasagne.

I haven't . . .

I watched carefully as the camera moved away from Monica Sitstill and showed an arena with little jumps and hoops and plastic tunnel-type things.

It was an obstacle course for dogs!

I used to love the obstacle-course race at sports day. We don't do it in Year Four, which I think is a TRAGEDY. It was my absolutely most favouritest race because you didn't have to be a good runner or a high jumper. You just had to remember which way round the course to go, and there were so many different bits to it: balancing bits, dressing-up bits, hopping bits . . . And this dog obstacle race was exactly the same! (Except I did notice that there was not

114

a dressing-up bit. But then I suppose it would be a bit hard to get a dog to wear your mum's trousers and welly boots. And probably a bit cruel as well.)

Those Boots are made for chewing.

'This course is the sort of thing pedigree dogs are expected to do at shows like Crufts,' Monica Sitstill explained. 'But on this show we are not interested in pedigree dogs. Our contestants tonight are all rescue dogs: strays or pets that, up till now, have had difficult lives where they may have been abandoned or even, sadly, mistreated by their owners.'

How DEVASTATINGLY awful, I thought. Honestly, some people just do not deserve to have the opportunity of being a dog owner. When I am as famous as Monica Sitstill I am going to make sure that only people who love dogs as much as I do are allowed to own them.

Monica Sitstill then went on to introduce the contestants. There were three different pairs, and frankly, even though the dogs were cross-breeds and strays, they were much more attractive in my opinion than the weird celebrities who were taking them around the agility course.

First of all there was a man called Geoffrey, who was very tall and had dark curly hair and apparently was some kind of celebrity from a show about cars, or something equally yawnsome. The dog he was paired with was very much more interesting. (Not that that would be difficult. After all, most things in life are more interesting than old men droning on about cars.) She was a beautiful scruffy wiry-haired dog called Teasel, with a very waggy tail.

Honey went
right up to the
telly as if to say
hello.

Teasel had been found locked in a shed on a
building site and hadn't been fed for weeks. It
was such a sad story I felt quite full of tears.

117

But Teasel was luckily much happier and healthier since the RSPCA had found her, so now she was all fit and raring to go on the agility course. I was beginning to get a bit fed up with Honey standing in front of the telly, but then she got bored of trying to get Teasel to play with her and came and sat back on the floor at my feet.

Why won't the tiny doggy play?

The yawnsome Geoffrey was very showy-offy and kept saying things like, 'Well, of course, training this hound will be a doddle after handling a supercharged Jaguar XKR.'

What a ridiculous thing to say, I thought. As if any man can train a jaguar. Everyone knows that they are wild and furious beasts of a terrifyingly dangerous nature.

How to Put a Brave Face on Things

Anyway, he was useless at taking Teasel around the agility course. Teasel was trying really hard, but Geoffrey kept walking the wrong way around the course, crashing into things, kicking the equipment and saying very rude words which the telly people had to 'beep' out.

Monica Sitstill quite obviously thought that Geoffrey needed a lot more training than Teasel. (That would make a brilliant programme: I would love to see Geoffrey being trained by Monica Sitstill to behave properly!) But she only showed her feelings in her face and did not say anything. In any case, she was much more interested in what Teasel was doing, and she gave a truly fantastic commentary:

'And here comes the lovely Teasel. She's approaching the jump. She looks a bit worried about it (who wouldn't be worried with a

119

trainer like Geoffrey . . .) But – aaah, look!
She's cleared it beautifully. No help from
Geoffrey; it seems he's too busy shouting and
jumping up and down, but never mind . . .
Let's see how Teasel does on the A-frame . . .
Remind me – what was that you said about
Jaguars, Geoffrey?'

The audience laughed at Geoffrey, which
made him say a few more beepy things. Then
they 'ooohed' and 'aaahed' at Teasel, and
I must say I did too, as she was so clever at
doing the course. She seemed quite pleased
with herself too, and barked in what I thought
was a very happy way every time she did
something right. And every time she barked,
Honey did too!

That tiny doggy is
so clever!

How to Put a Brave Face on Things

The coolest bit was
when Teasel did
the 'slalom'. She
had to weave in
and out of some
upright wobbly
sticks without missing
one out. She had to do it really
quickly too. It's a bit like those guys on skis
at the Winter Olympics who have to swerve
through poles without falling over. (Except that
Teasel didn't have to go downhill. And she
didn't have skis on.)

The whole course had to be done in as
short a time as possible. It was totally mega.
The audience clapped and cheered when Teasel
had finally finished. So did I.

Honey got really excited at all this
clapping and cheering and started rushing
around the sitting room wagging her tail rather

dangerously in the direction of the ornaments on Mum's coffee table.

Hey, I can run and jump and stuff too!

Monica Sitstill gave Teasel loads of praise, but told Mr Geoffrey Rude-Boy in her most fearsomest way to 'watch his language' in future. He actually did look quite scared, and did not answer back, I was pleased to see.

Then Ms Sitstill faced the camera and said, 'This kind of agility work – when done properly –' she glowered at Mr Geoffrey Rude-Boy – 'is an excellent way to develop a truly special bond with a dog . . .'

When she said this, it was like a penny dropping and the lights all coming on and I felt my brain actually have a real-life brainwave.

My brainwave was this: I would not be

going back to that horrid Mrs Woodshed and her obedience class (otherwise known as Public Humiliation Class). In fact, Mrs Woodshed could go and jump into a lake and take her huge Bosom and her moustache with her, as far as I was concerned. There would be no more obedience classes for me, oh no.

From now on I would train Honey on a One-to-One Basis. That way, we would be One Girl and Her Dog, and we would not need to ask for anyone else's help: not Frank's, not Molly's, not anyone's. Ever.

Look, I'm still running!

10
How to Come Up with a Masterly Plan

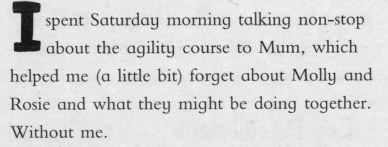

I spent Saturday morning talking non-stop about the agility course to Mum, which helped me (a little bit) forget about Molly and Rosie and what they might be doing together. Without me.

'If you helped me, Mum, we could set up a course in the garden and then I could do one-to-one training with Honey,' I told her.

'Why do you want to do one-to-one training when you are already taking her to obedience classes at the leisure centre? Mrs

How to Come Up with a Masterly Plan

Gritter is giving you a lift to the next one with
Frank and Meatball,' Mum said, not looking
up from her newspaper.

'Oh yes,' I said, brushing that comment
aside as I did not want to have to explain
about Honey's embarrassing incident with the
pee on the floor and how I could not suffer
the humiliating-ness of going back again. 'The
thing is, I've been doing some research and I
have discovered that it is much better to train
your dog in a one-to-one CAPACITY.' That
will impress her, I thought.

 Yeah!

It didn't.

Apparently Mum was not going to spend
her blinking weekend helping me to set up a

blinking course in the garden
so that no one could Rest and
Relax in the garden which is
what blinking gardens and
weekends are for. At least she didn't mention
the obedience classes again.

'Look, Summer, why don't you find a
friend to do this training with? I really don't
have time for it just now,' she finished with a
sigh.

I thought this was quite a harsh and unfair
thing to say, considering that Mum knew that
Molly and I had had a Falling Out and that I
was in need of love and attention.

I pointed this out: 'But I haven't got
anyone to do it with except you, Mum. Molly
is not speaking to me and no one else is
interested in Honey.'

Mum sighed and put her newspaper down
very slowly on the table and said in an extra-

gently-type manner as if she was making a big effort to be patient, 'Summer, I know you are upset about your argument with Molly. Listen, why don't you just ask her over to tea instead and not mention the agility thing?'

For a split of a moment I actually thought that my mum had come up with a good idea. Maybe if I involved Molly in my new project she would want to be best friends again. I was just about to thank Mum for her advice, when she went and ruined it by adding:

'And why don't you ask Rosie Chubb too? I expect she's a lovely girl really – she's probably just feeling a bit left out and trying to get your attention.'

I spent the rest of the weekend in my room on my own, drawing designs for agility courses and promising myself never

A-frame
↓

tunnel

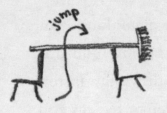

to talk to Mum ever again about friendship-related problems.

However, by Monday I had planned such an amazing course to set up in the garden that I decided I *had* to involve Molly. I was sure that as soon as I got a chance to properly tell her all about the breathtaking show *Pup Idol*, she would immediately forgive me for not taking her to the obedience class. Especially if I told her I was not going back anyway and that instead I was going to work on my own *Pup Idol*-ish agility course at home with Honey and that she could help me by being my Number One Special Advisor.

The only problem was, I had to get her on

her own before Rosie came and stuck to her like an oversized tube of superglue.

I raced into school with a big smile on my face and went to find Molly. On the way I planned carefully what I would say:

'Hey! Do you want to come round tonight for marshmallow-and-chocolate ice cream and we can set up an agility course together?'

And in answer to my most tempting and exciting PROPOSAL she would probably say, 'Does Batman wear pants over his tights?' which is Molly's way of saying 'without a doubt' – in other words 'Definitely.'

When I arrived in the playground I was OVER THE TOP OF THE MOON to see that Molly was alone. She was sitting on a bench and scribbling in a notebook in a very INTENT and concentrated manner, and there was no Rosie in sight.

'Hey, Molly!' I yelled as I ran towards her.

She looked up and started to smile as if she was pleased to see me, but then she frowned instead and looked down at her notebook again without even waving or saying hi.

I walked up to her and said, 'Did you see that great new programme on the telly on Friday—'

'Hi, Molly,' said an annoying squeaky voice. Hyena-Girl had sneaked up behind me. 'Is anyone bothering you?'

'Yes, actually, now you come to mention it,' said Molly, in a very posh voice as if she was an important grown-up teachery person who could not possibly be disturbed from what she was writing in her EXCLUSIVE notebook.

How to Come Up with a Masterly Plan

'There's a whiny voice coming from somewhere in front of me which is proving to be a distinct irritation.'

'B-b-but, Molly,' I stammered, 'I was going to tell you all about my new Masterly Plan for training Honey and ask if you wanted to help—'

'There it goes again!' Molly interrupted. 'Can you hear it?'

Rosie giggled and giggled her pathetic laugh as if Molly had just said the most hilarious thing in the history of all things hilarious when in fact even Frank Gritter has been known to come up with more comedic outbursts than this.

I stood there with my mouth hanging open. I knew it was not attractive, but I couldn't help it. My truest and bestest friend in the whole of the galaxy was not even going to say hello, let alone give me the chance to tell her all about my Masterly Plan. It felt like total and complete Public Humiliation.

I spent the rest of the day keeping myself to myself (which wasn't hard as I didn't have a friend in the world) and dreaming about how I was going to have to do Honey's training programme alone.

By the afternoon I had just about managed to get myself into an OK mood, when Mr Elgin made an Announcement that ruined everything again.

'Class – are you listening? **Frank?** **Well, please take your finger out of** **your nose** . . . Yes, I know you don't listen with your nose, but it's off-putting for me to have to look at you— Don't answer back! Right, everyone . . . I have an exciting announcement! As you know, every year, Year Four is in charge of raising money for a local charity. Well, this year it has been decided that you will do this by putting on a Talent Contest and selling tickets to your nearest and dearest. I suppose you are all acquainted with programmes such as *Seeing Stars* . . . ?'

Seeing Stars! That was one of Molly and my most favouritest telly programmes!

I tried not to think about the Days Before Rosie and forced myself to concentrate on what Mr Elgin was saying.

'. . . so I want you all to think carefully about what sort of an act you could do for the contest and let me know by the end of next week. We want singers, actors, dancers –' I heard Rosie whispering to Molly and they both started giggling – 'but if you've got an idea for something a bit more unusual, then let me know. All ideas are welcome at this stage.'

Then the bell went for last break.

This is it, I thought. This is my last chance

to make up with Molly – I'll get her to come round and plan an act for the Talent Contest.

I followed Molly out of the classroom, but it was no use. Rosie pushed in front of me and soon she was telling Molly all about her idea for a ballet dance for the contest, and how Molly would look 'simply gorrrrr-geous' in one of her pink tutus. Molly looked over her shoulder straight into my eyes, and as Rosie droned on and on I *thought* for one split of a moment that I saw Molly raise one  eyebrow in a QUIZZICAL manner that was a bit like my Dubious look. But when I tried to smile in an understanding and encouraging way, Molly suddenly stuck her tongue out at me and flounced off with Rosie.

Life was just so mega-unfair and horrible. Before Public Enemy Number One came on the scene, Molly and I would have LOVED

the idea of a Talent Contest. We would
have spent all our free time talking about it
and how we would win and be famous like
the people we used to talk about in our
Celebrity Club.

It seemed liked DECADES since we had
done our Celebrity Club.

I managed to keep my sadness inside
until the final bell rang, but then my eyes
immediately started doing the welling-up thing
and I had to run into the cloakrooms to hide
and try to stop them. I slumped down on to
one of the benches and put my head in my
hands.

Just my luck — Frank Gritter was in there,
getting his smelly footy kit from his peg. I
wished for about the ten millionth time that the
school would finally build a separate kit area
for the boys. If we girls had our own kit area
it would be clean and fresh and smell of spring

135

— instead of which in real life it smells of socks and dirt and snot.

'Hi, Summer,' said Frank, grinning from ear to smelly filthy ear. 'Coming to obedience class again tonight? Slipped in any puddles lately? Hahahaharrr!'

I sniffed loudly. I couldn't speak otherwise he would know that I was trying not to cry and that would be level one hundred and fifty on the mortification scale.

'Hey — don't do that! I . . . er . . . I was only teasing, I didn't mean to —' I peered up from under my mess of horrid tangly hair and through a wash of annoying tears I saw that *he* was the one who actually looked mortified.

'Just — go — away,' I said in a rather embarrassing hiccupy manner.

'Er, look, I didn't

mean to upset you,' he said, coming a bit nearer.

For one horrifying moment I thought Frank was going to put his arm around me! I edged away from him as his aroma threatened to ENGULF my senses. I thought I might choke, so I edged away a bit more. Unfortunately my edging had now brought me to the edge of the bench and I fell on my bottom with a crash.

I thought Frank would laugh at me like he usually does when anyone hurts themselves in such a comedic manner, but instead he said, 'Listen, I don't know about you, but I thought that class last week was pants.'

I know it is not a mature thing to do, but I always have to laugh when anyone says 'pants'. And even though I had been crying, I found that I was laughing now too.

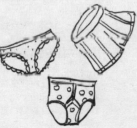

137

'And as for that Mrs Woodshed's Bosom,' said Frank. 'You could have put four wheels on it and called it a bus.'

Now I was laughing so hard I was almost crying again. 'Bosom' is another word that often sets me off. And the image of the bus was pretty hilarious too.

'And you know something else about that woman?' he continued.

I shook my head weakly.

'Well, she's obviously really a man in disguise,' said Frank, snorting with huge amounts of laughter too.

It was a funny thing – I had never liked Frank's jokes much before, but that day he was being mega-amusing.

'Listen,' said Frank, looking a bit more serious, 'do you want to go back to the obedience class tonight, or what?'

I shook my head again.

138

How to Come Up with a Masterly Plan

'Phew!' he replied. 'That means I don't have to either. I was only going cos Mum said I had to help you out.'

An idea was creeping into my head very slowly. I was not sure it was such a good idea, but it seemed a better one than waiting around for Molly.

'Frank,' I said, 'maybe you *could* still help me out. That is, if you wanted.'

I decided to tell him about my idea. After all, what had I got to lose? And as I told him, Frank started smiling again, and I thought maybe I had just come up with the Masterly Plan to end all Masterly Plans.

11
How to Build an Agility Course

rank came round after school with
Meatball and we announced to Mum
together that we were not going back to Mrs
Woodshed and her enormous Bosom. I had
told Frank that if he backed me up, Mum
would listen. And I had been right, especially
when Frank said (quite surprisingly and totally
UNPROMPTED by anything I had suggested):
'It would be a pleasure to help Summer train
Honey, Mrs Love.'

'Well, all right then,' Mum said in her most
begrudgingest manner.

And then Frank did a brilliant impression of Mrs Woodshed saying, 'Sit!' in a growly voice.

 Who said that?

Mum frowned and said, 'Hmm, I see. She does sound like a bit of a nightmare.'

'I never thought I would say this, Frank,' I said as we went out into the garden with some ice creams, 'but – thanks.'

Frank grinned and I think he went a bit red too, but it was difficult to see under all the footy-dirt on his face.

'So, what did you think about my Masterly Plan?' I asked him.

'Yeah, well, I don't watch *Pup Idol* and I've never done any of this agility stuff with Meatball,' he said, 'but if you think we can manage it, I say we give it a go. The only thing is, do you think Mr Elgin will mind if we bring our dogs into school?'

I rolled my eyes. 'It's for charity, isn't it? And he said he wanted "unusual acts" for the contest – well, you can't get much more unusual than two dogs doing an agility course in the school hall!' I said in an exclamatory manner.

'Yeah, all right!' said Frank, getting quite excited. Much like Molly's enthusiasm, my exclamatory manner can be quite infectious sometimes.

He finished off his ice cream and then we started setting up the course that I had spent the weekend planning. Mum had finally agreed that I could do this, as long as she didn't have to help in any way, and as long as I tidied up afterwards.

She had actually looked quite pleased when Frank had said that he would help me.

She'd even asked if he wanted to stay for tea.
I thought that was rather unnecessary and a
bit Over The Top, but I couldn't really say
anything now that he was helping me in the
Talent Contest. Especially if it meant that we
would go on to win and beat Molly and Rosie
in their 'gorrrrgeous' tutus.

We kept Honey and Meatball inside while
we set up the course. Meatball made a beeline
for Honey's basket and settled down for a
snooze.

Make yourself at home, Mum.

Honey followed us to the door, and when we
went out she watched us through the cat flap,
her long nose peeking out as if to say, 'What
are you guys doing?'

Can I play?

'We should start with a jump,' I said. 'What I need is a pole of some kind, and something to rest it on.'

'OK. Have you got a broom handle — that might work?' Frank suggested.

I had never realized that boys could be so helpful and, though I dare to say it, nice. We went to the cupboard under the stairs where Mum keeps all the cleaning equipment and had a bit of a RUMMAGE — which means we moved things around a bit to see what was there. Mum hates me rummaging in the broom cupboard so I had to be careful not to mess up what she calls her 'System', which means how she has put the cleaning products and things away. This seems to be to throw all the brooms against the back wall of the cupboard and then prop them up with buckets and tins of polish and piles of rags. It looks more like a Chaos than a System. But even in a Chaos like this,

How to Build an Agility Course

Mum always knows when I have rummaged too much, so I had to be careful.

Just as Frank and I had got everything that we needed from the cupboard and our arms were Full to the Brim with stuff, April came in through the front door. She had been at her office at Stingy and Gross or whatever it is called, and she made a big thing of plonking her briefcase down and sighing in a dramatical manner to show how tired she was after a day of flicking her hair and filing her nails and answering the phone in a posh voice.

'What on *earth* are you up to now?' she asked.

'Not much,' I mumbled, through an armful of brooms and buckets.

'Oh yeah?' said April in her sarkiest of tones. 'Does your boyfriend always go around with cobwebs in his hair, then?'

Boyfriend?

'Come on, Frank,' I hissed, avoiding contact with his eyes in case he went along with the whole 'boyfriend' idea and said something to embarrass me further. 'We've got work to do.'

Frank followed me back out into the garden and helped me prop up a broom on

146

two garden chairs so that it looked like one of
the jumps on the telly. We made a couple of
jumps like this. Then we made a seesaw with
a plank of wood balanced on a log. For the
tunnel, we got my old nylon collapsible tunnel
which used to be tied on to a tiny plastic
climbing frame when I was a baby. Now it
was kept in the toy box which, embarrassingly
I still had in my room. Lastly, we stuck a
load of bamboo sticks into the grass to make
a slalom like on *Pup Idol*. It looked really
professional!

'Just one thing,' said Frank. 'How will you
do the slalom in the school hall?'

I tutted and rolled my eyes to give myself
time to come up with a good answer, as I had
not thought about this. 'We'll use Blu-Tack or
something. Honestly Frank – you really must
learn to think Laterally instead of Literally.' I
don't think he understood, as he just shrugged

147

and helped me stick the last bamboo cane into the grass. Then he said, 'Right, I'll go and get Meatball.'

'No, not yet,' I said. I was quite enjoying doing some bossing around for a change.

'Why?'

'Cos we have to train one dog at a time, or it will be Utter Mayhem,' I said importantly. 'And as it was my idea, I think *I* should start with *my* dog first.'

Yeah, Ladies First.

Frank huffed a bit, but he agreed in the end, especially when I said he could have another ice cream. While he was getting it from the kitchen, I got Honey and called her to come to the first jump.

Monica Sitstill had said, 'The maximum height of the jump should be as tall as the dog's shoulders.' I measured Honey against the broom on the chairs and realized that the jump was a little bit higher.

'Never mind, Honey,' I said. 'Monica Sitstill probably meant that was how high the jump should be for those rescue dogs on *Pup Idol*. They've had a much more deprivational life than you, so they are probably not as fit. You are a pedigree dog, so I'm sure you can jump higher.'

 Whatever you say!

Honey will normally do anything for a bit of food, and I knew from watching *Love Me, Love My Dog*, and reading the book too, that treats were the best thing to use when training dogs. So making my voice sound Full of Authority, I faced Honey and I told her, 'Honey – lie down.'

149

Pup Idol

As I said 'lie down' I showed her a treat which I then hid in my fist. Then I lowered my fist to the ground. Honey followed the treat with her nose, which made her nose go level with the floor, and then she lay down completely at which point I gave her the treat as a reward.

I like this game!

'You *are* a clever girl!' I said. 'Now, you can have another treat if you do a jump for me.'

I made her stay where she was, then I walked around the jump that I had set up and, holding another treat up high I called out: 'Jump!'

Honey looked at me in a puzzled kind of way with her head on one side, and then she sprang up on her HAUNCHES (that is,

her back legs) and for
one JOYOUS second
I thought she was
going to clear the
jump.

But instead she
came crashing
through the
broom, snatched
the treat right out
of my hand with her teeth, and flung me to the
ground, pinning me down with her front paws
and licking me all over my face.

Frank of course came back outside at that
very moment and laughed his face off in a
rather unhelpful manner.

'OK, you do it then,' I said sulkily. He was
most obviously not used to being in any way a
Team Player.

Frank still had half his ice cream in his

151

hand, so he put the whole thing into his stinky mouth in one go and swallowed the lot in the way that only a show-offy boy can do.

It turned out that he was not any better at getting Honey to do the jump though. He tried about a thousand million more times, but she kept crashing through it to get the treat. We both got fed up with her and told her off.

First you give me a treat, then you shout at me . . . Make up your mind!

'OK, let's try something easier,' Frank said eventually.

'Yeah — what about the A-frame?' I suggested. The A-frame was a sort of high-up walkway that we'd constructed out of three planks of wood so that it looked like a giant

'A'. HENCE, as Molly would say, the name
'A-frame'. Bit obvious really.

Anyway, the A-frame turned out to be
even more of a truly calamitous disaster than
the jump. Honey would not walk up it at all.

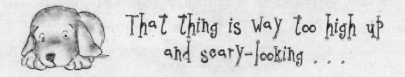

That thing is way too high up
and scary-looking . . .

In the end, I climbed up it myself and held out
a treat to see if she would come on with me.

The treat idea worked, er, a treat! Honey
did follow me, but unfortunately it was in
quite a boundsome manner, and all the
bounding and pounding on the planks of wood
meant that the A-frame became rather wobbly-
ish and then quite a bit more wobbly and
then, just as Honey reached me and the treat,
the whole thing collapsed in a heap with me
underneath it.

'Help! Frank! Help! Honey's squashing me!'
I screamed.

To make matters worse, Meatball suddenly
appeared from nowhere, saw the heap of
planks and Honey going crazy doolally and,
with a leap of delight, landed right on top of
us.

Hey, Mum! Join the fun!

How to Build an Agility Course

'Frank!' I screamed again. 'Why did you let Meatball out?'

Frank did not reply. He was helpless with laughter. Eventually I managed to wriggle and get my head out, so that I could at least breathe.

'Har-har-har!' Frank was actually roaring with laughter now, hopping around and pointing at us. 'Now *that* is something we should work into the act! We could dress you up as a clown and then we'd be bound to win!'

I wanted to say something suitably cutting and sarcastic and clever to shut up his stupid laughing and wipe it once and for all from his dirty, idiot face, but just at that moment Honey and Meatball's rough and tumbly game sent them crashing into one of the jumps in our carefully laid-out agility course and then they went crashing through the seesaw and the slalom poles, until they had wrecked everything. I ran after them, screeching at them to stop and succeeded in being thoroughly ignored.

What a Blast!

Frank did not help at all even a tiny bit. He did not try and stop them and he did not try to save the agility course. He just laughed.

So much for my Masterly Plan.

I told Frank in No Uncertain Terms (which means I made it very clear indeed how I was feeling, which was sore and angry) that I would no longer Require his Assistance for the Talent Contest.

'You are of no use in helping me to train *my* dog, and what is more it seems that you cannot even control your *own* dog.' I said this with my hands on my hips and my nose in the air.

How to Build an Agility Course

'Suit yourself,' said Frank, which was not the reaction I had been expecting, I must admit. I had thought he might at least say sorry. 'Do your stupid agility course on your own. I've got a much better idea for the Talent Contest anyway.'

And he stormed off, taking Meatball with him.

Oh, I was just getting into the swing of things . . .

So that's all the thanks you get for agreeing to let a boy come to your house and for giving him, not one, but *two* ice creams.

12
How to Make Up After Falling Out

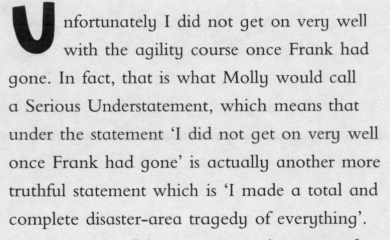

nfortunately I did not get on very well with the agility course once Frank had gone. In fact, that is what Molly would call a Serious Understatement, which means that under the statement 'I did not get on very well once Frank had gone' is actually another more truthful statement which is 'I made a total and complete disaster-area tragedy of everything'.

The truth of the matter was that none of my rehearsals for the Talent Contest got any easier the whole of that week. Whatever I did,

How to Make Up After Falling Out

Honey just did not seem to understand the tricks
I wanted her to perform. I kept holding out
treats and repeating the commands, just like they
did on *Pup Idol*, and she kept running at me like
a cow in a shop full of china cups and then she
would knock me flying and take the treat.

Food, glorious food.

The final straw came on Friday, after yet
another long week of being ignored by Molly
and giggled at by Rosie.

I got home and decided to have one last
attempt at training Honey to go through the
tunnel. I led her out into the garden and made
a big fuss of her.

'Honey, if you do this for me, I promise I'll
get you the biggest, juiciest chew that pocket
money can buy.'

She seemed to understand that I was being

serious, because she put her head on one side and her big brown eyes looked right into mine as if she was really listening to me.

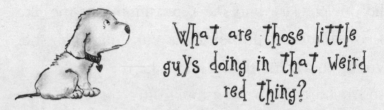

What are those little guys doing in that weird red thing?

'Honey, where are you— HONEY! STOP!'

She had not been listening to me at all. She had been looking at Cheese and Toast, our two lazy cats.

'HONEY!'

They had gone for a snooze in the tunnel and Honey had decided to pounce.

Got to strike while the going's good!

Honey always made the mistake of thinking

the cats wanted to play with her. It was always a very BIG mistake.

But the little guys want to play hide-and-seek . . .

Honey hared into the tunnel after the cats, who started making a huge hissing noise, which normally means 'Don't come near if you value your nose'. When that didn't stop Honey, the cats decided to escape and zoomed out the other side of the tunnel in a streak of black and white, like a pair of cartoon moggies. Unfortunately, Honey tried to escape after them, but she was too big to shoot quite so easily through the tunnel.

She got stuck.

Does my Bottom look Big in this?

And as if this wasn't bad enough, she carried on running even though she was stuck.

So now there was a red tunnel with a golden head and a golden tail, running around the garden, chasing after Cheese and Toast.

Now the little guys want to play 'tig'!

Cheese and Toast are not the brightest of cats in the history of FELINE intelligence, and instead of running into the house or up a tree to get away from Honey-the-Moving-Tunnel-Dog, they panicked and jumped on to the seesaw. Honey then leaped on to the seesaw too, which made the other end ping up violently, and of course this sent the cats flying into the air.

Cheese seemed to glance in horror at Toast as they were both catapulted in an arc across the length of the garden while Honey kept chasing after them, still firmly wedged into the red tunnel.

I grabbed the hose, turned it on and started chasing after all three of my crazy pets, as I thought this might stop them in mid-tracks. But

163

it didn't, so I screamed 'STOP!' at the top of my lungs instead.

It was no good. It was very bad, in fact — total complete badness and Mayhem.

I flumped down on to the grass and burst into tears.

And then I heard someone laughing. Oh great, I thought. Mum has come out to laugh at my latest disaster. She's probably brought April and Nick and half the neighbourhood with her. After all, I am such a comedy show of hilarious Proportions. Or maybe, even better, Frank the smelliest boy in town has come back to GAWP and tell me again what a mega-clown I am.

Slowly I stood up and turned to see . . . Mum and . . . oh no! Molly. She *would* have to come round at this precise moment and be a Witness to this total Disaster and Calamity, wouldn't she? I thought, How am I going to talk my way out of this one? She is never going to want to be friends with me now that she, like Frank, has seen what a clown I have become. She will go into school on Monday and tell the whole class what a waste of space I am and how I am never going to win the Talent Contest in a million years with my pathetic dog-show idea and . . .

I had forgotten that I was still holding the hose, and as I was thinking these sad thoughts I suddenly realized that Molly and Mum were getting completely soaked . . .

Before I had time to panic and think that this was turning into the nightmare of all nightmares, Molly shouted, 'WATER-FIGHT!' at the top of her lungs and flew at me with a full watering can.

I was now soaked right through to my skin.

Molly was giggling so much I thought she

165

might possibly split both of her sides in true
life.

Even Mum was laughing.

'This is MEGA!' Molly squeaked, and
grabbed a bucket which she filled with water
and threw over me as well.

Mum then grabbed the hose off me and

showered me and Molly until we shrieked and screamed, 'STOP!'

At last Mum turned off the hose and, still laughing her whole face off, she went inside to get us some towels.

'We haven't had a water-fight for like AGES!' Molly said, throwing her soaking wet arms around my soaking wet neck.

I didn't know what to say to that. We hadn't hugged each other for ages either. In fact, there wasn't *much* we'd done together for ages.

Molly seemed to know what I was thinking and looked a bit embarrassed. Then she said, 'Is this, er, your act for the contest?'

'Erm . . .' I said.

'I mean – getting cats and a dog to do a circus act with water – now *that* is what I call entertainment!' she said.

I thought for one a tiny split of a moment

161

that Molly was being SARCASTIC again – in
other words, mean and unfriendly – and I
was about to say something rude back about
wearing 'gorrrrr-geous' tutus and hanging out
with Public Enemy Number One. But then
Molly started giggling again and pointing
at Honey. I turned to see a very bedraggled
pooch, still wedged in the tunnel, looking
very pleased with herself. And then I started
laughing too and Molly and I fell

into a heap on the grass next to Honey, and we giggled until we couldn't breathe.

It looked like our Falling Over had stopped our Falling Out.

It's the water-fight – works every time.

Mum came back out into the garden with towels and a change of clothes and a large banana and strawberry smoothie for each of us.

'It's great to see you girls having a laugh together,' she said. 'Listen, Molly – why don't you give your Mum a call and see if you can stay for a sleepover tonight?'

Mum can be really cool every once in a while, when she puts her mind to it.

Pup Idol

'Will you stay?' I asked Molly.

My best friend wiped the laughter tears from her eyes and said, 'Does Romeo love Juliet?'

In other words: 'Just try and stop me.'

13
How to Get Inspiration

Molly and I sat on the grass after Mum had gone back inside.

'It's great that you're staying over,' I said, trying my hardest not to sound all that excited about it, even though my tummy was doing the churning butterfly thing that it does when I'm over the top of the moon.

'Yeah,' said Molly, staring at the grass.

Then a bubble of happiness found its way to the surface of my body and I squeaked out a giggle again, and Molly took one look at me and she squeaked out a giggle too, and there we were, a couple of loonies, rolling around on the grass, laughing our faces off together all over again.

Honey thought this looked like a huge load of fun.

Mind if I join you?

Tunnel-dog came lolloping over to us.
'Ow! Honey! Get off!' I yelled, as my mad pet rolled on top of me and the sharp wire bits of the tunnel frame dug into me.

This set Molly off laughing even harder, which was not all that helpful in the circumstances.

'Molly – get this hound off me!' I cried, pushing Honey as hard as I could.

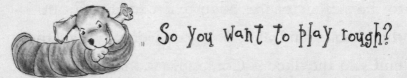

So you want to play rough?

At last, I'm pleased to say, my best friend did

pay some attention to the seriousness of the
situation and we both managed to get hold
of the back end of the tunnel and pull it off
Honey.

Honey was so pleased to be free, she did a
VICTORIOUS lap of the garden at such a top
speed that her back legs tried to overtake her
front legs and she did a somersault into what
was left of the A-frame and knocked it flying
into Mum's lavender bushes.

Free at last!

Luckily Mum was not looking out of the
window. She flips the top of her lid off when
Honey crushes the lavender.

We recovered from another giggling fit and
then Molly said, 'So, you and Honey really are
entering the Talent Contest with this agility
thing, then?'

Molly was being quite persistent about wanting to know what I was doing, I noticed. She was also using her Nonchalant voice – which means she was trying to pretend she didn't care what I was doing for the contest. I was sure I could see the corners of her mouth twitching a bit. Did she think it was a funny idea? I felt rather a bit indignatious at that, and I was going to say something like, 'Well what extra-clever and special thing are you and dear Rosie Chubb doing then?'

But I decided better of it, and instead I said rather clippedly, 'That is the definite plan, yes. So are you entering the contest?'

'Er – yeah. Of course,' Molly answered. I thought maybe she sounded a bit unsure, which was weird. I mean, at this Stage of the Game, with the contest only two weeks away, you either were going to enter into the Running or not.

How to Get Inspiration

'So?' I tried asking her in a PROMPTING way to get her to tell me more, 'what are you doing then?'

Molly stared at the grass again. 'Rosie and I are doing a dance.'

'Oh,' I said. And I stared at the grass too. It was just typical of Rosie to get Molly to do this, as Molly was a super-mega dancer and could easily win *Seeing Stars* with some of the routines she has come up with in the past; whereas Rosie is Chubb by name and chub by nature in my opinion and most probably looks like a HI *ppo* in her 'gorrrrr-geous' tutu. Although that may be being unfair to hippos.

Molly sighed very deeply and said, 'Have you got any ice cream?' which I took to mean that the subject was well and truly closed for the moment.

175

Pup Idol

She followed me into the kitchen, and as I put a double scoop of Chunky Choc Chip into a cone for Molly I tried to think of something else to talk about, because she had gone very quiet. Then I had an idea: maybe I could show her a bit of *Pup Idol*! I had recorded the latest programme, as I had missed it that week, so I asked Molly if she would like to watch it with me.

We have always enjoyed watching telly together, and when I told her that this programme had celebrities in it doing the dog handling, she did seem to cheer up a bit, as Molly loves the whole celebrity thing even more than I do.

So, later on, Molly and I settled down in front of the telly with a large bowl of toffee-flavoured popcorn and some drinks to keep us going through the excitement of it all.

How to Get Inspiration

Honey sat with us – though not on the sofa, as she is not allowed. She sat on the floor at our feet, wagging her tail.

 I love watching those tiny doggies – But how do they get in that Box thing?

Shame she doesn't seem to have picked up any tips about how to perform like a perfect pooch.

The first celebrity contestant on the programme was a singer called Charisse that I did not know much about, but Molly recognized her from one of her magazines.

'*Look* at that dress!' she said in an exclamatory way. 'It's to *die* for!'

What on earth was that supposed to mean? Who in their right mind would want to die for a dress? Personally I thought the singer was totally UNSUITABLY clothed for the occasion of dog handling. She was wearing heels that were far too pointy and tall, like big dangerous knitting needles, and her hair was long and floppy and kept falling into her eyes. She was actually a bit like April, the way she kept flicking it everywhere.

As I'm sure it is needless to say, her routine did not go very well. The dog that she was looking after was a huge big thing like a cross between a wolfhound and something else monster-ish, and he obviously liked the hair-flicking more than any of the treats the lady had in her hand. Every time she flicked her hair, the dog jumped up and put his paws on her shoulder and tried to lick her face. It freaked me out as it made me think of Nick Harris when he had his beard, and then that made me think of him kissing April, which is a thought I do not like to think.

Molly loved the whole show though. She

kept laughing and pointing and talking about everything and soon I was doing the same, and at last we really were back to being how we used to be.

The best bit of the show was what happened at the end. It was incredible beyond belief. A man in a shiny suit came on the stage with a lovely black and white dog who was a collie crossbreed (it was a little bit like those sheepdogs that were in the film about the pig called *Babe*). Monica Sitstill was doing her thing of talking about what we were going to see on our screens next, and she was explaining that the man was a professional dog-handler, so I thought maybe he was going to show the celebrities how they ought to have handled their dogs. But no! It was even more amazing and wondrous than that.

Some music started playing in the background. It was kind of thrilling, slightly

spooky music like they use at the beginning of films like *Mission: Impossible*. And then the lights in the studio went down and there was a spot of light on the man and a spot of light on the dog. And then . . . THE MAN STARTED TO DANCE WITH THE DOG!

Nice dog! Shame about Mr Shiny-Legs though.

How to Get Inspiration

First of all the man walked backwards, and the dog followed him, crouching right down as if it was sliding along the floor on its tummy.

Then the dog went up on to its hind legs and danced backwards, and the man walked forward towards it.

Then the dog looked to the side and the man looked to the opposite side, and then they kept doing this in time with the beat of the music.

And then – the best bit ever – the dog, back on all fours now, danced through the man's legs, round and round, weaving in and out, using the man's legs as if they were actually slalom poles!

And at the end the dog bowed! It really did! It bowed its head and lowered the front of its body to the ground to Accept the Applause.

And it got a *lot* of applause.

And a lot of treats, I noticed . . .

'That programme was the wickedest programme in Wickedsville!' said Molly, when we were getting changed into our PJs. 'Why didn't you tell me about it before?'

I stopped in mid-PJ-putting-on and said in a shocked way, 'But I did try.'

'When?' Molly asked.

'It was in the playground when you were talking to Rosie,' I said. 'And you both pretended that you couldn't hear me.'

Molly's face went red very quickly. She looked as though she was going to cry. She hardly ever cries. Only when she gets hurt, like when Rosie Chubb actually stuck a pencil in her arm (I wished she'd remembered *that* particular incident before she had decided to be best friends with Public Enemy Number One)

and when one of the boys put a frog in her hair in Year 2. And that was years and years ago. But I couldn't understand why Molly would want to cry now when we were having such a great sleepover.

'Yeah, well, Rosie can stuff it,' she said quietly.

'WHA—?' I was shocked.

'You heard me,' said Molly. 'She's not my friend any more. That's what I came round to tell you earlier, before the water-fight and everything. In fact, Rosie never *was* my friend. She's boring and all she talks about is tutus and pirouettes and — and — and she can't even dance.'

Ah. That would be a bit of a problem if you were planning to do a dance for the Talent Contest.

Molly looked at me from under her fringe and said, 'I'm sorry, Summer. I've been horrible

183

to you. I was just so upset that you went to the obedience class without me.'

I felt *my* face go red then and I stammered, 'I-I know. And I'm sorry too because I should have let you come with me. It's just that the rules said only one person per dog, and I didn't know how to tell you, because I knew you'd get upset. And also, I'm sorry to say this, but I did think I would get on better with Honey on my own because I thought that it would be the way to be truly Bonded as a Pair with her. But it turned out I was wrong,' I added, feeling a bit SHEE*p*ISH – that is, embarrassed, not white and woolly.

Molly smiled. 'Let's forget about it. We're friends again now, aren't we?'

I hugged her (I had put my PJs on properly by now). 'You betcha.'

Molly breathed in deeply and hugged me

back and then she said, 'So what are we going to do for this Talent Contest then?'

I must have looked a bit surprised at this last comment because it was honestly not a comment that I had been expecting.

'Er – *we?*' I said.

Molly grinned. 'Well, I'm not going to enter with anyone other than my Best Friend, am I?'

'Oh,' I said. 'What about Rosie?'

'I told you – she can't dance. And seeing as it was a dance that we were supposed to be doing together, I think I'm better off out of that idea, don't you?'

'Right,' I said.

'Plus,' Molly added, getting into a bit of a stride on the subject of 'being rude about Rosie', 'she knows Zero-the-Hero about celebrities. How lame is that?'

'Yeah,' I said.

'So,' Molly continued, 'like I was saying –
what are we doing for the contest?'

I hesitated, as I didn't really know how to
say the next bit.

'Er, Molly, the thing is . . . You may
as well know . . . Honey's not exactly been
performing well in the agility training. I don't
think I'm going to be entering the contest at
all, to be honest.'

'I see.' She looked as glum as I felt and we
both stared at the floor for a while.

Then she looked back at me and I saw
that her eyes were doing the kind of sparkling
gleaming thing that they only do when she has
come up with a Masterly Plan.

'How about a bit of a rethink?' she said in
her most craftiest of mannerisms. 'How about
we combine our talents?'

I wasn't sure I was following this line of
thinking.

186

How to Get Inspiration

'You know – I can dance, you've got the dog . . . Do I have to spell it out for you?'

And then it clicked.

'We'll enter as the DANCING DOG DUO!' I shouted in an Alliterative manner.

'Well, trio,' Molly corrected me.

I was so happy, I didn't even want to argue.

14
How to Work as a Team

The next day I woke up with worries and doubts jumping around inside my mind. What if Honey was as bad at dancing as she was at everything else?

Who's Bad?

What if she did not behave and drove Molly crazy? What if Molly stormed off like Frank had done?

I didn't want to say any of this out loud though, especially when Molly woke up with a big grin on her face and said, 'Today's the day, Summer Love! Today we start our training programme!'

And so Molly and I spent the whole of Saturday and every spare moment after that training Honey.

You guys wear me out!

In between the training, we still had to go to school and do homework. I had really had enough of school. The weather was getting to that stage where it's too hot to be sitting in a classroom. Our school buildings are extremely ANCIENT, in fact I think they are Antiques. They were obviously built in the Ice Age when the sun didn't shine very much, as they are clearly designed to keep you as warm as possible. This means that when it is very hot you feel as though you are like a sausage in a very high temperature of oven. That is,

189

SWELTERING. But because it is school and there are lots of Meaningless Rules, you must still wear proper clothes that are too hot and make you sweat, instead of something sensible like a swimming costume.

If I ever become a teacher (which I severely hope I will not, as that would be Social Death) I will make new rules that say that classes will finish in May and not RESUME until October. During the terms, if it does get too hot, classes will be served outside with a side order of ice creams and cooling drinks and there will be water fountains to run in and out of at Convenient Intervals. All pupils will be required to wear swimming costumes and delightful hats to keep the sun off their faces and out of their eyes.

On top of all the heat and the sticky plastic chairs and fully-clothed-ness, I was fed up with Public Enemy Number One trying to get back

in between me and Molly, and with Frank Oh-How-He-Stank Gritter making pathetic remarks about my lack of dog-trainership ability.

If only he knew! We were actually getting along rather well with things. This was mainly because Molly has always been the cleverer one in our partnership of best-friend-dom, and she came up with the idea of finding out about dancing dogs on the Internet.

'Hey, look at this, Summer!' she said when we were round at her place one afternoon, sucking on ice pops to try and keep ourselves from melting. 'Did you know that there's a posh expression for describing what we are trying to do? It's called "heelwork to music".'

On the website there was loads of info about this, because it is something that people do at Crufts every year! I also found out that there was once a puppy in true real life called Honey who won a competition at Crufts a few years ago called 'Pup Idol'! How weird is that? That must have been where the telly programme got its idea from.

'We should call our act "Pup Idol"!' I said. 'Every act in a Talent Contest has to have a name, and I'm sure Crufts and the telly people won't mind. After all, it is for charity.'

'A truly STUPENDOUS idea indeed,' said Molly.

In other words, brilliant.

And so with the use of the top tips from the Internet, Molly began to make one of her lists, which she says are INVALUABLE, which means they are totally and absolutely necessary. She wrote down what we needed for our training programme;

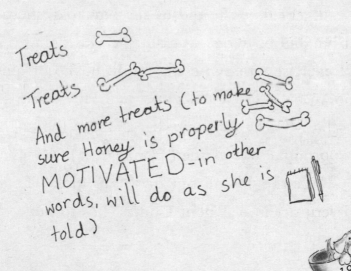

Treats

Treats

And more treats (to make sure Honey is properly MOTIVATED–in other words, will do as she is told)

Paper and pen (to plan routine)

Costumes (must be classy)

Music (must be ATMOSPHERIC, that is dramatical and mood-Setting)

With all this planned, we started our training sessions. We taught Honey to 'SCOOT' (that is, to *walk backwards*), and to go 'UNDER' (that is, to *crouch down* and squeeze under one of those limbo poles), to *wave* by saying 'PAW' and to walk on her *hind legs* by saying 'UP'.

Every time she did as she was told, she got a handful of treats. Luckily she was doing a lot of exercise, otherwise she might have got quite porky!

Got to keep my energy levels up!

How to Work as a Team

I found everything was so much easier with Molly around. For example, sometimes Cheese or Toast would get in the way in the lazy manner they do, which is to lie around on the lawn in just the place that we wanted to do some training. Honey would always try and chase the cats instead of concentrating on the routine, but Molly came up with a plan.

'Don't worry,' she said. 'I'll grab the cats and put them inside while you hold on to Honey and give her a treat. That way she'll come to associate treats with staying still and not chasing the cats.'

Those little guys are sweet, But the treats are sweeter.

Also, if Honey ever did something wrong, Molly would remind me, 'Remember what Monica Sitstill says: "Reward the good and

ignore the bad!"' This meant we should ignore
Honey every time she did something wrong
and only make a fuss when she did something
right.

If Molly hadn't been there, I would have
got in a fluster and given up far too easily.

We really were a great team.

Yes indeedy!

Finally the two weeks were up and it was the
day of the Talent Contest. I had not been able
to eat even one crumb of my breakfast because
my tummy was full to the brim with butterflies
and probably other kinds of creepy-crawly
things as well, judging by how I was feeling.

'Summer, you must eat something,'
Mum said as she slurped her coffee.

'Why?' I asked grumpily. 'You're not.'

'Don't answer back, Summer,' Mum

snapped, which is what she always says when she knows that I am right and she has not got a leg to balance on.

I ignored her nagging and went to check over Molly's list yet again for the thousand millionth time to see that I had got everything I needed for the contest.

Molly's mum had been brilliant as usual

and had helped us get the Classy Costumes
together. She has always kept fantastic old
clothes that the family don't want any more
in a huge trunk in the attic. It has dresses and
hats and cloaks and jackets and even things
like walking sticks and funny shoes in it. If you
push your hands right in deep, you can feel all
kinds of interesting things that have fallen to
the bottom and sometimes you pull out surprise
things like big red clowns' noses or funny pairs
of glasses that are way too big — once I even
found a wig.

Anyway, we weren't wearing clowns' noses
or wigs for our dance. (I could just imagine
what Frank Gritter would have to say about it
if we did . . .) Mrs Cook had found a couple
of old black leotards on to which she had
sewn some stars made from scraps of silver
SHIMMERY fabric. Then she had lent us
each a top hat that had been used in a play

she had been in hundreds of years ago when she had been young. She had cleaned them up and stuck a band of the shimmery fabric around them so that they matched Effortlessly and Elegantly with our leotards.

'You will wipe the floor with the opposition!' she had declared when she saw us in our costumes.

(I didn't like to say anything as she had been so helpful and nice and I didn't want to seem rude, but I had no intention of doing any floor-wiping – or any other kind of cleaning – at the Talent Contest. I was going to have fun, and housework of any sort was not going to come into it.)

Honey and I were getting ready in the back room at home.

'Are you ready?' Mum asked, coming to find us.

199

April was behind her. 'Do we really have to sit through this dross?' she asked in her usual oh-so-charming manner.

'April, you know how hard Summer and Molly have worked for this contest,' Mum said.

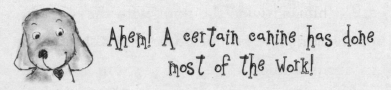

Ahem! A certain canine has done most of the work!

'And Honey!' I added, giving my pup a tickle under the chin. I didn't want Honey to get offended at this DELICATE stage of the proceedings. She might go off into a mega-huff and not perform. I did not want everything to go melon-shaped at this point.

Mum drove us all to school. I left Honey with her and April while they parked the car, and I went into the hall where the Talent Contest was going to take place. Mr Elgin was busy putting the finishing touches to the stage and the seating arrangements. Lots of Year Fours were in the hall including, to my utter dismay, Frank Gritter – with Meatball!

'What are you doing with Meatball?' I asked him.

He grinned in that outrageously annoying fashion of his and, as if he was announcing a circus act, he yelled, 'Roll up, roll up! Come and see the amazing Mr Frank Gritter and his fabulously obedient and talented dog, Miiiiiiiiiss Meeeeeatbaaaaall!' And then he bowed before an imaginary audience, that is, me.

I rolled my eyes in the most extravagant way I possibly could to show him that I thought it was a load of rubbish. But inside I was QUIVERING. Frank was doing an act with Meatball! What was I going to do? Molly had told me very firmly that no one else would be COURAGEOUS enough to

201

do an act with a pet. And when Honey saw
Meatball, she'd go crazy doolally just like she
did at the obedience classes. Just like she did
when she saw ANY other dog, let alone her
mum.

I had to tell Molly about this truly
disastrous calamity and try and get us out
of the contest before it all went horribly
wrong and we made utter foolish fools of
ourselves.

I turned to run and find my best friend and
hurtled straight into –

'Summer,' said Rosie Chubb. She was
almost snarling. 'I want a word with you. Not
only have you stolen my best friend Molly, but
you've stolen my idea for the dance as well!'
she hissed. A bit of her spit landed on my nose,
which rather detractivated from her attempt at
looking fiercesome, I thought.

How had she found out? We had kept it a

secret from everyone except Mr Elgin! He had promised not to tell anyone.

This was turning into a day of Hellish Proportions.

15
How to Be a Pup Idol

I ran into the school car park to find Mum and tell her to take Honey home right away.

'There you are, Summer!' Oh no, it was Molly and her mum and dad. 'Where is Honey? You have remembered your costume, haven't you? Actually it doesn't matter if you haven't cos Mum—'

'We can't do it, Molly,' I blurted out.

'What do you mean?'

'We can't do this contest with Honey and the dance!' I shouted in a bit of a tearful manner.

'What's going on, Summer?' Mum and April had appeared with Honey. At the most Inconvenient Moment, of course. Honey was already looking very excited.

I'm ready for my fifteen minutes of fame.

I took a deep breath and told them about Frank and Public Enemy Number One, who was at that very second eyeing up my guts to use them as garters (though what she would do with garters is a mystery to me. No one wears them these days.)

'I cannot believe that you are letting a show-off like Frank Gritter get to you!' Molly cried. 'He does not stand a chance in a squillion with his silly mutt.'

205

'Hey! That's Honey's mum you're talking about!' I said.

You tell her!

Molly pursed her lips at me like she does when she wants to tell me that I am totally missing the point. 'As for Rosie,' she went on, 'she's much more angry with *me* than she is with you, because I told her to her face that she was a useless dancer and that I'd rather dance with a dog than groove with a goofy-faced gerbil like her.'

'Molly!' said Mrs Cook.

'No one speaks about my Best Friend the way Rosie did, and gets away with it,' said Molly.

Don't — you're embarrassing me.

My heart expanded so much that I thought it might burst out of my chest in true life. (That was rather a terrifying PROSPECT as I didn't want an ambulance called in to make this whole day even more of a chaotic disaster scene.) I decided there and then that I *would* do the show. How could I not, when my Best Friend was one hundred and ten per cent on my side?

'Come on then, Molly!' I announced. 'What are we waiting for?'

Molly grinned. We linked arms and, leaving Honey tied up outside next to Meatball, we went into the hall to get ready for our act.

Hi, Mum!

Once we were changed into our classy leotards and matching top hats, Molly and I took our places at the front of the audience with the rest of our year. Then Mr Elgin walked up to the stage and spoke into a microphone:

'Welcome to Year Four's Talent Contest! Thank you for coming. The children have been working hard on their acts, and we have a vast array of different talents to share with you. Without more ado, let me introduce the first act. A big round of applause, please, for Miss Sophie Block and her puppets!'

I have to say, it was probably the most direst of dire acts to start the show with. Sophie Block is the youngest in the year, and she is really quite immature and babyish and still likes playing with dolls a lot. And her so-called 'puppets' *are* actually just over-big dolls. And they are ugly. And Sophie's act was just her talking to her dolls in a squeaky sicky voice and telling them stories like 'Goldilocks and the Three Bears'. Really quite yawnsome.

There were a few more equally truly awful acts along the lines of people playing recorders and standing on their heads for five minutes (not at the same time though) and I was beginning to think that maybe Honey, Molly and I would have the tiniest chance of winning.

Then it was Frank's turn with Meatball.

What can I say? They were truly faberoony. Meatball was the obedient-est pooch in the history of pooch obedient-ness, and Frank had total control over her. She sat when he said 'SIT', she rolled over when he said 'ROLL OVER' and she gave him her paw when he said 'PAW'. Needless to say, there was loads and loads of clapping and cheering after this.

'Well, that's that,' I said under my breath. 'We will Pale into Insignificance next to Frank and Meatball.'

I slumped back into my seat to ENDURE – in other words, put up with, the next act which was . . .

'. . . Rosie Chubb performing some ballet,' Mr Elgin's voice was beginning to take on a rather wearisome tone of speaking.

Rosie came on stage in a pink fairy outfit. She looked out into the audience until she had found me and Molly and glared very hard at us in a distinctly un-fairylike way, I thought, and then she did a curtsy. And then – oh dear – she began to dance to some music

which she had brought along on a CD player.
It was the most lamest of lame dances I have
ever seen in my whole life. She fell over when
she tried twirling in what Molly whispered was
'supposed to be a pirouette'. Then she leaped
into the air and landed in a crumpled heap
on the floor. And then she skipped across the
stage like an elephant in wellies and fell over
her own huge feet. But she just did not stop
dancing. She carried on and on making a total
and utter SPECTACLE of herself.

I should have been pleased. But as the
dance went on (and on, and on) some people
in the audience started to snigger and giggle,
and I found that I was actually feeling quite
sorry for Rosie. After all, she had thought that
Molly was going to be doing the dance with
her.

But Rosie had still gone on and danced
alone.

Even though, as Molly pointed out, she had the talent of Your Average AMOEBA.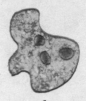

And then someone in the crowd started laughing really loudly, and Rosie's face went a dark pink colour, which looked quite bad against the fairy tutu, and even from where I was sitting I thought I could see her bottom lip wobble. This made me feel quite outraged. Couldn't they see that she was doing her best and actually being quite brave, getting up on stage in front of about a hundred people and dancing (well, falling over mostly) like that?

What I did next was really very strange when I thought about it afterwards. But at the time I did it without thinking.

I ran outside, grabbed Honey, then ran back inside and grabbed Molly. Then I marched them to the front of the stage and I pressed the stop button on the CD player.

How to Be a Pup Idol

Molly was pulling her hand away from mine and hissing at me, 'What *are* you doing?'

But for once I was not going to worry about what my Best Friend was thinking. I knew that I had to do the Right Thing.

I put our CD of Atmospherical Music that we had chosen for the contest into the player and walked up to the flabbergasted Mr Elgin and took the microphone from him and had a quiet word: 'Trust me on this,' I said. (I have to say he didn't have a very trusting look on his face, but I wasn't going to be Put Off at this stage.)

I tapped the microphone in a professional manner and said, 'Ladies and Gentlemen, a big round of applause for Rosie Chubb who has just done a wonderful job at introducing the main part of her act, which is in fact: PUP IDOL!'

213

And then I started whooping madly with excitement (and Deranged craziness) and Honey started leaping around the place, and the audience seemed to think something very interesting was about to happen and so they all whooped as well.

 It's time to rock and roll!

While everyone was clapping and cheering loudly, I BECKONED with my finger for the girls to come closer and I whispered: 'Rosie – you're a great dancer. Just improvise to the music I'm about to put on. Molly, go ahead as planned.'

'But Summer—!' Molly tried to get a word in, but I just gave her the kind of look Mum gives me when she wants me to do as I'm told.

I settled Honey and told her to 'LIE DOWN' and gave her a treat.

214

Treat-time again!

Then I pressed play on the CD player, and Rosie stood in one of those ballet positions called something like demi-first-plié-position and even managed not to fall over, and Molly crouched down in her starting position for our dance so that she was facing Honey, and I crouched down on the other side of Honey, and the music started.

We had decided to use the *Mission: Impossible* music that they had used on *Pup Idol* as it was the most atmospherical music we could think of, and it meant that we could copy some of the moves we had seen on the telly.

The music started in that creepy way it does: ♩ *der,* ♩ *der,* ♫ *der-der,* ♩ *der,* ♩ *der,* ♫ *der-der,* ♩ *der,* ♩ *der,* etc, etc, and so on. Honey was watching Molly very intently indeed — well, the treat in Molly's hand, anyway, and as Molly moved backwards in time to the music, Honey moved forward, as if she was sliding along on her tummy.

Eyes on the prize . . .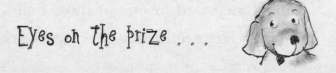

Then I called 'Honey!' and she leaped round, almost doing a spin in mid-air as the music got faster and more exciting. I held a treat up to get Honey to put her paws on my shoulders and we danced like a couple of people at a ballroom-dancing competition.

At that very moment in time I suddenly felt like the proudest person in the world. Honey was looking right into my eyes and even though her tongue was hanging out and she was panting for England, her eyes seemed to say to me, 'I'm pretty proud of you too, Summer!'

If I can just get that treat . . .

Was this it? Did this mean that we were at last well and really Bonded in true life?

Give me the treat, and I'm Yours forever!

Then Molly broke the Tension of the moment because we'd got to the part in the routine where she had to call Honey and hold her cane/walking-stick thing out like a pole for the high jump. In her other hand she held a treat, so Honey's eyes and nose followed the treat . . . and then

Honey did it! She jumped higher than she'd
ever jumped before!

Little Biscuit, here I come!

I was a bit worried that she was going to
crash into Molly – or Rosie, who was still
doing some weird kind of ballet-twirling behind
Molly.

(Rosie seemed to have taken me very
seriously when I said 'improvise' and she was
now tiptoeing around the stage with a grim
look on her face as if she was a baddy in the
film *Mission: Impossible* and was being followed
by a policeman, except that baddies don't
generally wear pink tutus.)

In any case, I didn't have time to DWELL
on what Rosie was doing, as Honey had
actually landed beautifully and was now
running in a loop around the stage and making

her way back to me. I held my cane/walking-stick thing quite low and parallel to the floor and showed Honey a treat and said, 'UNDER,' and Honey scooted under the cane, keeping her body close to the ground.

Such fun!

Then she went behind me and I said, 'UP,' and she put her paws on my shoulders and looked into my eyes again, and Molly ran around behind us and beckoned to Rosie who was still doing her weird baddy-in-a-tutu routine, and the four of us stepped forward in time to the music, turning our heads from side to side as if we were all baddies looking out for policemen coming to get us.

Then the music ended and we all turned to face the audience and Honey dropped down on to all fours.

Phew!

There was a split second which felt like about five hours during which nothing happened. The whole hall was completely silent.

It was like that moment at the end of *Seeing Stars* when you are waiting to hear who has actually won, but they make you wait and wait to Build Up The Sense Of Anticipation. It was almost unbearable the way the air was filling up with all this Tension. I could almost smell it – unless that was Frank's socky whiff wafting out towards me.

My heart started beating at top speed and volume so that everyone must have been able to hear it and possibly even see it bumping around inside my chest. I thought I was going to die right there on the spot. And then a voice shouted, 'WHOOOO-HOOOOO!'

I looked to see who it was: it was Frank

Gritter. He was climbing up on to his chair
and clapping his hands wildly, and as he
climbed up, all the other ninety-nine people
in the hall whooped as well and clapped and
shouted 'Encore!' (a French word which means
'You're so fab — please do your act again')
and everyone was yelling and stamping their
feet and climbing on their chairs.
Someone even threw a plastic flower
at me, which I decided to take as a
compliment, although I thought it
was a pretty weird thing to do.

And then Mr Elgin came on to the
stage. He looked quite stern: his eyebrows were
knitted together into one black spiky caterpillar
and he was frowning over the top of his
glasses, and I thought, Here we go. Summer
Holly Love, prepare yourself for the biggest and
hugest telling-off of your life right here in front
of one hundred people.

221

He picked up the microphone from the side of the stage where I had left it and said, 'Words fail me.' (Except they most obviously didn't, because he then went on to say some more.) 'Judging from the unanimous reaction of the crowd, I think I need say no more than, "Congratulations, Summer, Molly and Rosie!"'

'And Honey!' Frank shouted.

'. . . and indeed Honey,' said Mr Elgin, doing a bad job of disguising a grin that was escaping from the corners of his mouth. 'That act has to be the most original I have ever seen . . . and so the winners of the Year Four Talent Contest are . . . Miss Love, Miss Cook, Miss Chubb and Miss – er – Honey Love!'

I shook my head. It couldn't be true. We all bowed and hugged each other (except Honey, of course). I even hugged Rosie, and she sort of hugged me back.

222

Then Mr Elgin gave us each a medal. Even Honey got one.

Afterwards people kept coming up to us and slapping us on the back and saying how fantastic we were. Frank Gritter came up to me too.

'You did it, Summer!' he said. 'I never thought I'd see you get Honey to do anything that she was told, but you definitely did it.'

I was still feeling quite overwhelmed and puzzled by everything.

'Yeah, er, thanks, Frank,' I said. 'And, er, I'm really sorry you and Meatball didn't win. And I'm sorry about being bossy to you and getting cross when you came round to my house.'

Molly butted right in at that point. 'EXCUSE ME!' she shouted. 'You had FRANK GRITTER round to YOUR HOUSE? And you didn't TELL ME?'

223

Frank grinned even more widely than a wide-mouthed frog.

Luckily Mum appeared at that point and said, 'Do you want to ask all your friends back for a celebratory tea tonight, Summer?'

I looked at Molly, whose mouth was still wide open in shock at the thought of Frank being a friend of mine, and I looked at Rosie, who didn't seem to know if she had any friends at all, and then I looked at Honey and Meatball, who were rolling over and over each other in a mad-dog frenzy, and I said, 'Yeah, thanks, Mum. That'd be really great.'

And so that is how I, Summer Holly Love, learnt to Progress My Relationship to a New Level with my dog, Honey . . . and my best friend Molly.

It is also the story of how I made some new quite surprising and thoroughly unplanned friendships with Rosie Chubb and Frank Gritter.

I think you're forgetting someone . . .

And with Meatball too, of course.

And it's how Honey won the completely and truly deserved award of being a fantastically brilliant PUP IDOL!

I'll Be signing autographs Backstage . . .

Agility Course

A-frame:

Honey to balance along the
plank like one of those
circus people on a rope that
is tight.

A-frame
↓

↑ tunnel

You've got to be kidding!

See-saw:

Honey to walk up the see-saw and balance
while it tips down on the
other side.

What's in it for me?

Slalom poles:

Honey to run in and out
of these poles without
knocking them over.

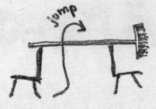

slalom

Says Who?

Jump:

Honey to jump over this
and fly through the air
with the Greatest of
Ease.

jump

It's YOU who'll Be
taking the running jump
around here . . .

TOP of the PUPS

The PUPPY PLAN

Anna Wilson

When Frank's Labrador had puppies, I knew I absolutely HAD to have one of them for myself. It took a lot of Being Persistent, but finally Mum said YES and we chose Honey! However, being a caring pet owner is actually Quite Hard. There's the WEEING on the floor and the CHEWING of shoes — not to mention the fact that my big sister, April, has a cringesome love crush on Honey's vet . . .

The first hilarious, barking-mad adventure in the Top of the Pups series

PUPPY Power

TOP of the PUPS

Anna Wilson

Now my pooch, Honey, is a bit older, life as a dog owner has become rather *yawnsome*. The only dramatical event in the house is my big sister, April, BLUBBING about her yucky-lovey-dovey crisis with her boyfriend. But I have come up with an OVER-THE-TOP faberoony plan to bring some excitement back into our lives. All I need is for Mum to agree that Honey can have PUPPIES!

The third hilarious, barking-mad adventure in the Top of the Pups series

Puppy PARTY

TOP of the PUPS

Anna Wilson

I was over-the-top-of-the-moon when my big sister, April, FINALLY moved out, but then Mum went and put me in charge of planning a surprise birthday party for her. It's utterly not fair as it's Honey's birthday the same week. But my Bestest Friend, Molly, and I have had a Masterful Plan: we are going to have a fantabulous joint dog-and-human birthday party! Puppies, party food, games — what could possibly go wrong?

The fourth hilarious, barking-mad adventure in the Top of the Pups series

THE GREAT KITTEN
CAKE OFF

Anna Wilson

'READY? STEADY?
WHAT ARE YOU WAITING FOR? . . . BAKE!'

Ellie Haines despairs of her family. Her brother is obsessed with getting on TV, Mum is going through some kind of midlife crisis, and Dad's bad 'yolks' have reached alarming 'egg-stremes'.

The only bright spots in Ellie's life are her naughty kitten, Kitkat, and her best mate, Mads. But when Mads and Ellie apply for The Junior Cake Off, their friendship soon starts to crumble. Can Ellie win back her best mate, or will their friendship go up in smoke?

DO YOU LOVE ANIMALS TOO?

If so I'd love to hear from you. Write to me at:

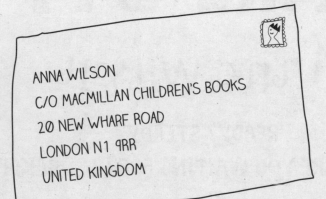

ANNA WILSON
C/O MACMILLAN CHILDREN'S BOOKS
20 NEW WHARF ROAD
LONDON N1 9RR
UNITED KINGDOM

Remember to enclose your full name and postal address (not your email address) so that I know where to write back to! And please do not send me any photos or drawings unless you are happy for me to keep them.

Anna xxx